# InSight

By James Wittenborg

INSIGHT



ISBN 979-8-218-11386-5

Cover design by Rob Bignell, Inventing Reality Editing Service

Manufactured in the United States of America
First printing December 2022

# Prologue

She looked to be three, perhaps four-years-old. Her wavy brown hair blew wildly in the wind, as she raced up and down the driveway, pulling the red wagon that carried her three favorite dolls. Content in her own little world and focusing only on the safety and comfort of her dolls, she remained under the watchful eye of her mother, except for that brief moment.

The tree-lined street that invites residents to take walks or lounge on front porches was quiet, except for the sounds of wind-blown leaves flapping high up in the trees. Chalk lines faintly visible in the street marked the end zones for the after-school football games. The only strangers who ever drove down this street were the ones in search of homes for sale. They never found any.

One morning in late October, the peaceful innocence of Colbert Drive would change forever. An old white van driving slowly through the neighborhood would have appeared to be oddly out of place had anyone noticed. But on that morning, the strange vehicle rolled up and came to rest at the end of the driveway at 716 Colbert Drive. The van's door flew open, and the lanky figure sprinted half-way up the driveway to the young girl gripping the handle of her wagon. She barely made a sound, as she was whisked away.

# Chapter 1

Colbert Street was tucked in the back of a heavily treed subdivision where vehicle traffic was never an issue for the neighborhood kids who used the street as part of their playground. The old white van cruising through the streets would have seemed out of place, had anyone noticed. No one did. There was little activity on the block on this overcast, breezy morning, except for young Jennifer Sears play-ing in her driveway under the watchful eye of her mom, Loretta.

Ryan Field just stood there in open view beside the driveway of this neatly landscaped home, only a few yards from where Jennifer was playing. Loretta Sears was sitting in a chair just inside the garage assembling Halloween decorations when something inside the house drew her attention. After a quick glance at Jennifer, she abruptly turned and disappeared into the house.

Ryan's eyes were drawn to movement in the street as the van silently rolled to a stop at the end of the driveway. He stood frozen in place and watched the figure emerge from the van. He was perhaps six feet tall, slender, shaggy brown hair tucked under a worn Yankees baseball cap, dark blue T-shirt, and jeans. And, although Ryan stood mere feet away in plain sight, the stranger running up the driveway didn't seem to notice. Ryan simply watched as the stranger swiftly grabbed the young girl, carried her into the van, and quickly sped away.

Seconds later, Loretta Sears appeared from the garage clutching her 8-month-old baby, who had just awakened unexpectedly from a nap. She had been in the house for no more than 90 seconds. Not seeing young Jennifer, she frantically called out her name, as she ran to the front of the yard. Tears flooded her eyes as she let out a desperate scream. Still clutching her infant daughter, she turned and quickly ran to the garage to find her cell phone. For ninety

seconds, she took her attention away from her little girl. It took just less than
ninety seconds for the driveway abduction to occur.
Ryan Field slowly walked down the driveway to the street, glancing back to see a hysterical mother on her phone pleading for help. A red wagon with three bushy-haired dolls sat motionless in the middle of the driveway. A blank stare in the direction of where the van disappeared, he vividly recalled the description of the stranger who took the child, details of the van, and the North Carolina license plate number he had seen. As he turned back toward the house, the scene around him began to melt away and was replaced by the sound of voices and a piercing light. He opened his eyes and rolled over to avoid the morning sun streaking through the partially opened blinds. His wife, Lisa, and the boys could be heard chattering in the kitchen, already devouring breakfast.

# Chapter 2

The morning routine was always the same. Lisa Field never relied on an alarm clock, her robe and slippers at the side of the bed, and always first in the kitchen to prepare breakfast. Ryan's hand would generally pound the snooze button, however on this morning, it was the kitchen jabber that woke him up. He laid there a moment, stared up at the ceiling, then rolled out of bed and into the shower. As soothing as the strong stream of hot water felt, it just couldn't relieve the soreness moaning from the muscles in his back and shoulders. He thought that heading back to the gym yesterday after work would be a fresh start on getting back in shape. Yet, as Ryan has had the tendency to do too many times in the past, he pushed a little too hard in a desperate effort to make up for lost time, suffering the con-sequences of his no pain, no gain mentality. He was a year shy of forty and barely hanging on to that high school athletic physique he had as a teen.

Ryan threw on a pair of sweats and towel-dried his hair, as he followed the strong smell of bacon coming from the kitchen where thirteen-year-old Jason and ten-year-old Aaron sat finishing their breakfast. Lisa turned from reading her morning paper when she heard Ryan enter.

"Good morning stud!" Lisa said with enough sweet humor to mask the sarcasm.

"Morning Dad," the boys chimed in.

Lisa turned her attention back to the *Fulton Times*, spread open on the table. Her long brown hair was pulled back in a ponytail and at thirty-eight years old, was as pretty as when she first met Ryan on the campus of NC State where she languished as an accounting major. Lisa had only attended college at her parent's insistence, however, in her sophomore year she shattered her ankle in a skiing accident and subsequently dropped out. She remained out of school long enough to lose all interest in ever going back and, because her dad was the town's certified public accountant, wound up working in his office during tax season.

"Coffee's on the counter and there's also some muffins here on the table," she said, turning her attention back to the morning paper. Ryan gave up a long time ago trying to pretend he was a health nut when it came to eating. He craved his sweets in the morning, especially her homemade muffins.

"Nasty article today about wasting taxpayer dollars on some proposed rail system nearby." And then with that devilish grin, she added, "You know anything about that?"

"Really? This early in the morning you've got to start with me already? I've been on this rail project for almost three years and have been hearing these types of remarks almost on a daily basis. Let's be thankful that for now, it remains the governor's pet project and as long as he's in office, I've got a job...and we've got an income!"

There was a certain enjoyment shared in the exchange of verbal jabs every now and then; it always kept things lively. Lisa turned the page and continued reading when her mood suddenly changed. "Oh my!" she said, gasping at the paper.

Ryan noticed the serious tone of her voice. "What is it?"

"A young girl was kidnapped yesterday on the other side of town." Lisa glared at Ryan in disbelief. "Why?" she said as her voice trailed off.

"Did they provide any more details?" Ryan asked out of curiosity, not making any correlation to the dream he'd had.

"Her name was Jennifer Sears, and she's three years old. Here's what I just don't understand...the little girl simply disappeared while playing in her driveway. Where on Earth were the parents? Who was watching her?" There was anger in her voice.

Lisa's eyes welled with tears. He recalled a story she had told him about her childhood years ago. When she was 12 years old, a classmate was kidnapped while walking home from school and never found. Lisa was so affected by it that she became fearful of going anywhere alone or without a familiar adult somewhere nearby. It also explains why she has always been so protective of their two boys.

Ryan knelt and wrapped his arms around her. As he held her, his eyes drifted to the article on the table...*little girl...disappeared ...while playing in her driveway*.

# Chapter 3

Aaron sprinted up the stairs after dinner that night to set up the video game he had borrowed from a friend earlier in the day. "Hurry Jason! And bring some chips up with you!" Aaron barked, as he neared the top of the stairs.

"Start without me, dad's going to give me a hand with my bike," Jason shot back as he wrestled on a sweatshirt and headed for the garage. Ryan was already there waiting when Jason walked in.

"So, what's the problem?" Ryan asked gesturing to the 10-speed bike leaning against the back wall.

"I don't know, it's not changing gears the way it should. When I turn the shifter knob, nothing happens." Ryan walked over to the workbench and fumbled around with a few screwdrivers and a wrench, before finding what he was looking for.

"I think the cable just needs to be tightened up a bit," Ryan said without turning around.

"Dad, is it *this* cable? When I...Dad?"

Ryan's head snapped back as if cold water had just been thrown on him. He looked at Jason, and then the bike. "Sorry son," he said sheepishly. "Ya know, I think you've got a handle on this."

Jason could see that his dad's attention was on something else and thought it best to just call it a night. "Yeah, I think I know what to do," Jason lied. "I'll work on it tomorrow." He walked slowly back into the house while Ryan remained in the garage.

Lisa looked up from emptying the dishwasher and could see Jason's face, as he walked through the door. "How's the bike coming along?" she asked.

Jason tried to disguise his disappointment. "I think we have a plan for fixing it."

Lisa sighed. "Is your dad in there doing it for you?" Ryan had a bad habit of trying to fix everything without involving the boys.

"No Mom. In fact, dad seems a little distracted tonight. I don't know, maybe he's tired."

Ryan's mind was stuck on the previous night's dream as he aimlessly walked around the garage. The more he thought about it, the clearer the details aligned with what Lisa read to him this morning. *Could it just be a wild coincidence and why was the dream still so vivid*? He shook his head and walked over to the workbench where he put away a few stray tools and tidied up. He realized he was getting nothing done in the garage, so he turned and headed back to the house.

"You ok?" Lisa asked as he entered. "Jason said you seemed a little distant."

"Fine, just a little tired. Got a lot going on with work right now." And with that, he turned and walked to his office. This was his man cave. While most people considered a man cave to have wide screen TVs, sound systems, recliners, and perhaps a wet bar, Ryan preferred his cave to feature well-stocked bookshelves, walls plastered with pictures, articles of great transportation accomplishments, and his prized mahogany desk. It wasn't exactly an atmosphere to entertain friends and Lisa always respected Ryan's privacy when he chose to retreat to his "cave."

Ryan shut the door and settled into the tall leather chair, clasped his hands together, and stared at the blank computer screen. As he sat there, random scenes, in great detail, played out in his head, though they were not from the previous night's dream. *A dog running, a woman riding a bicycle on campus, and a red Mustang.* As this scene faded, another emerged of a baseball field and a storm. It was all vaguely familiar, but he wasn't sure when or from where. Or...could these have been in his dreams as well? The longer he sat and thought about them, the more vivid the details became, and the more disturbed he felt about them.

Lisa was down the hall in the family room, stretched out on the couch, thinking about how odd Ryan's behavior was. First, Jason tells her that his dad didn't seem too eager to help with the bike, then, he walks in and admits to being tired and goes straight to his office and shuts the door. He'd disappear into his "cave" occasionally during the week when he had a few deadlines to meet for work, but seldom did he ever seclude himself in there on a weekend. No, something's not right, she thought as she stood outside the office door. Lisa thought a freshly brewed cup of coffee might help, and it would certainly give her a reason to see how he's doing.

# Chapter 4

Earlier that same day, Sergeant Joe Ramos arrived for his 8 a.m. shift at the Fulton Police Department. Fifteen years on the force, Sgt. Ramos was considered one of the old-timers in the precinct. At five foot, ten inches, thickly built with a wide toothy smile, he looked more like a guy you'd find tossing pizza dough in the air at Luigi's rather than one of Fulton's men in blue. Regardless, he was a recognizable figure in the community, not only for his police work, but also for his countless hours volunteering and tutoring students.

Six years earlier when his wife died of cancer, there was a tremendous outpouring of support from Fulton's citizens, business owners, and community leaders. Whenever he walked the streets, citizens would approach with a smile and give him a hug. Well-wishers streamed into the station house to see him or to drop off flowers or food baskets. He never had children and considered Fulton his "family," however there was one thing his family could never know about him.

Sgt. Joe Ramos harbored a very deep, dark secret.

One night, eighteen years earlier, Jose Ramos Alvarez illegally crossed the southern border into the United States along a remote, thinly guarded area of Arizona where those desperate to enter found little resistance. For several years, he had been a small-time criminal and occasional drug runner, making drug drop-offs in the States several times a year. And although he was good at it and the demand for his services was on the rise, Jose Ramos Alvarez was having a change of heart. He had watched too many of his friends die or get caught and knew it was only a matter of time for him. He wanted out. So, on a cool February night he packed some clothes and with a few dollars in his pocket, made his move and slipped across the border.

Jose Alvarez slipped in and out of the shadows for several days until he landed in a small town that was home to several dozen others in a situation like his. They were all toiling in a hot warehouse, working for almost nothing, but they were fed, had a place to sleep, and were hidden from the authorities. Jose Alvarez stayed just long enough to save a few dollars for a ride to Tucson. There, he found work at odd jobs and made a connection to procure paperwork documenting him as Jose "Joe" Ramos from Tucson. His intent was to use this new identity in a place as far from the southern border as possible, so he headed east, eventually landing in the suburbs outside of Raleigh.

He worked hard at every opportunity given to him, always wore a smile, and kept a low profile. Sometimes, on days he didn't work, he'd just take a walk through the busy downtown streets of Raleigh and enjoy the freedom of his new home. The pleasant sun and crisp air of a Raleigh springtime seemed to invigorate the diverse community of college students, businessmen, retirees, and the young families moving into the area. Joe Ramos would smile at anyone and everyone, and people would generally smile back. Joe Ramos felt alive in Raleigh and wanted more. He wanted to be what they were, a part of the community.

His paperwork and easy charm were enough to get him in the door and enrolled at a community college where he wound up taking two years of courses in public safety. During those two years, he could be seen volunteering in soup kitchens and with the Salvation Army. One day he walked into a Raleigh station house inquiring about opportunities to become an officer. A young Hispanic officer greeted him in the lobby, and they spoke for nearly an hour. He told Joe Ramos that, unfortunately, there were no openings and many applicants on a waiting list. But he knew of a small town south of Raleigh that might be looking for a few officers. The next day, Joe Ramos made his way to Fulton.

In the years that followed, Joe Ramos was a model citizen who got married, continued his education, and became a pillar in his community. However, despite the passing of nearly two decades, the fear of being caught never went away.

***

"Good morning, Sgt. Ramos," said one of the new recruits looking up from his desk.

"Good morning, Tyler." Sgt. Ramos made a point of knowing people's names, especially the new recruits. He connected with everyone. Before he could get to his office though, he was intercepted by the wiry-framed Sarah Bunning. Sarah was the "everything" person in the precinct: dispatcher, secretary, supply manager, basically, whatever was needed, she took care of it. She was even relied upon to repair the copy machine.

"Joe, I put a fresh stack of cases on your desk," she said. "There might be a few more later this morning."

He gave a wry smile and sarcastically replied, "Thanks Sarah, but I really would have preferred a coffee and Egg McMuffin instead." He then broke out in that famous toothy grin.

"Yeah, well, maybe tomorrow if you're nice to me." They exchanged a smirk, but it was a sure bet that tomorrow there would be a fresh cup of coffee and Egg McMuffin on the desk of Sgt. Ramos when he arrived in the morning. Sarah did more than hold the office together; she always seemed to do the little things that kept morale high.

On his worn wooden desk, there sat a neatly stacked pile of manilla folders representing the open cases Sarah had delivered. Grabbing his coffee mug, he walked to the break room and drained the remainder of a nearly empty pot. He could feel the eyes of the office coffee vultures tracking him, waiting for him to make the next pot. Once made, the vultures would swoop in, fill their mugs, but leave just enough to not have to make the next pot. Joe Ramos just took it in stride. Full mug in hand, he returned to his desk to get down to business. As expected, the vultures swooped in the moment he left the breakroom.

The first few folders contained citizen complaint cases, standard stuff. Then there was the break-in at the Ace Hardware store three weeks ago that was still going nowhere. Midway through the pile was a folder with a red star in the upper corner. The red star folders usually signified the cases that were a bit more egregious and urgent. He opened that folder and focused immediately on the word *abduction*. He was very familiar with the abduction of Jennifer Sears and had been following the story on the news. The file contained no scribbled notes added, no handwritten markings on the forms, nothing. No leads at all.

# Chapter 5

Lisa pushed open the office door. "I just made a fresh pot and thought you might be interested." The steam rose from the cup as she carefully walked it over and set it down on a coaster, a safe distance from his laptop. Ryan never turned around but maintained his quiet stare at the screen while his fingers rhythmically tapped the desk.

He glanced to his side at the mug. "Thanks hon. There're just a few things I need to do and then I'll be back out there with you." But she had already left the room. He leaned back in his chair, closed his eyes, and pressed his memory for those two specific scenes that raced through his mind earlier. He began to drift off into a light sleep as he recalled the hit and run incident.

*Wispy clouds reflected the orange hue of sunset. Old trees lining the street provided cover for the cars parked like sardines in front of small, box-like student residences. Ryan didn't recognize the area, but it appeared to be a college campus. He found himself standing on a sidewalk observing a light brown dog as it ran across a nearby yard toward the street. He looked away from the dog to see a woman on a bike riding in the street toward him. A car's engine can be heard coming up the block. The dog sprinted between two of the parked cars and into the street. The car slammed its brakes and swerved to avoid the dog but veered into the path of the woman on the bike, knocking her off and throwing her into a parked car. After a brief pause, the car drove off, leaving a lifeless body in the street.*

Ryan opened his eyes and took a deep breath. He quickly grabbed a pen and scribbled down a few notes on what his mind just played back. He leaned over the keyboard and began an internet search.

*Hit and run...woman on bike...college campus.*

The search yielded numerous results that mostly keyed on the term *hit and run*. Article after article described horrific details of various hit and run accidents, however, none seemed to fit what his mind saw. This changed the moment he scrolled to the next page. The third story down was *College Student Dies in Hit and Run*. Ryan sat up, felt his heart pounding, and inhaled deeply as he leaned in closer to read.

She was a 20-year-old junior at NC State, and her name was Allison Tate. The article stated she was killed in a hit-and-run on Boylan Street near campus on Tuesday, Sept. 17, at around 7 p.m. There were no witnesses or arrests, and the case was still under investigation. Ryan continued reading through a few dozen additional hit-and-run articles but none of them were as close to his dream as the incident at NC State. He printed the article and placed it in a folder in the bottom drawer of his file cabinet.

A car horn honked out front, breaking the silence in the room. This was shortly followed by a stampede of feet down the stairs, a shout yelling goodbye, and the slamming of the kitchen door. He was still trying to comprehend what just happened. When he calmed down, the thought of the other dream came to mind about a baseball field and a storm. He pushed the chair back away from the desk, leaned back, and closed his eyes. Quiet, deep breaths brought a relaxed state as he thought of nothing except the ballfield and the storm.

*Ryan walked into a park that contained multiple baseball fields specifically designed for youth baseball games. He recognized the area as the town he grew up in many years ago. Two games were in progress on adjoining fields. It wasn't raining, but the sky was growing dark as thick, black clouds began to move in. Parents seated in the stands nervously watching the sky as they continued to cheer for their kids on the field. Rain was sure to come, but until that first drop fell, there was no need to stop the game... And then the bolt struck. The sudden white spear of light struck in the outfield, selecting a frail 11-year-old, as its path to ground. Pandemonium*

*ensued, as young players and parents ran to each other, while all those around me scattered, leaving behind*
*a prone figure lying in the grass.*

Ryan's eyes slowly opened, and he leaned forward and placed his palms on the mahogany desk. There was no doubting now what was happening. He didn't bother to write down any notes; he just placed his fingers on the keyboard and began his next search.

*Lightning strike...ballplayer...Hicksville, NY.*

Ryan's search immediately resulted in several articles, all citing the same event. Eleven-year-old Benjamin Payne was struck and killed by a bolt of lightning while playing centerfield during a little league game at Hicksville's Dutch Lane School. There was no need to read any further. These events had actually happened, and Ryan was *there*. He printed the article and placed it in the folder with the other one. He then turned off his laptop and sat, wondering what it all meant.

# Chapter 6

Ryan's drive to work the next morning was a blur and before he knew it, he was seated at his desk with a steaming Styrofoam cup in his hand. He was jolted from his thoughts by a voice.

"Are you coming?" came the question directed at him from the hallway.

Ryan jerked his head up to see Joe Farrell standing at his door.

"The big guy hasn't arrived yet, but it would be nice if we were all in there when he does!"

Ryan looked at his watch – 8:35. He quickly grabbed a notebook and jumped out of his seat. He had never been late to the eight-thirty meeting and would probably have forgotten about it altogether if not for Joe's friendly reminder.

"You all right? You look a little lost," Joe said with a concerned look.

"Just lost track of time, that's all," Ryan said as the two continued down the hall.

After the meeting, Ryan slipped back to his office and shut the door. He reviewed an architectural drawing for several minutes, then pushed his chair back from his desk and stared up at the ceiling. All he could think about was the abduction of that little girl, the woman on the bike, and that young boy on the ballfield. The thoughts persisted until it was time to go home.

Friday, the routine was more of the same; seclusion in the office, no interaction with co-workers, and little attention given to work. Ryan ventured out of his office only to retrieve his lunch from the breakroom or attend mandatory meetings, where he uncharacteristically sat in the back, away from the discussion. This did not go unnoticed by his colleagues, and the buzz around the office was that there might be some personal issues at home. Meanwhile, Ryan's family sees the same behavior at home and attributes it to the stress of his job.

***

Saturday morning rolled around, and the Field residence was unusually quiet. Jason and Aaron's only plan for the day was to sleep late. At 8:15, Ryan rolled over to see Lisa sound asleep, so he quietly peeled back the covers and crept out of bed.

"You're up early," Lisa said without lifting her head from the pillow. "It's Saturday, why don't you just stay in bed for a while? I'll get up soon and make us all a nice breakfast?"

Ryan leaned over and kissed her on the cheek. "Didn't mean to wake you. I just can't sleep anymore." She groaned and rolled back over on her side, content to stay put. He then walked over to the dresser, found a pair of neatly folded sweatpants, slid each leg in, and headed to the kitchen, quietly closing the bedroom door behind him.

*Did I really dream those events, or could I have read about them at some time and simply forgotten that I had read them? Maybe I've seen them reported on the six o'clock news, and they simply lodged themselves back in my brain somewhere.* Ryan sat at the kitchen table exploring every explanation that might make sense of those scenes in his head and their correlation to real life events. The morning caffeine was stimulating his brain into high gear.

He walked to the kitchen junk drawer, searched for a notepad and pen, and lumbered back to the table to rehash his experiences. First, the abduction. He had a vivid dream, walked into the kitchen, and was read an article by Lisa that appeared in the local newspaper that morning. Next was a dream about a woman being hit by a car that was later confirmed in a search of the internet. Then, a third dream about a young boy being struck by lightning, which was also confirmed on the internet. Ryan racked his brain hoping to find a common thread that somehow connected the three, but they were all so different with nothing apparently in common.

*The abduction.* Ryan recalled that it took place somewhere on the other side of town. He jumped out of his chair and ran to the family room where the week's newspapers were kept until they were picked up with Monday's trash. He located Thursday's Fulton Times and opened it to the page detailing the abduction of Jennifer Sears. Scanning the article, he found what he was looking for; *716 Colbert Drive in Fulton.*

Ryan snuck in and out of the bedroom to retrieve a pair of jeans and a sweatshirt. Everyone in the house was still asleep as he slipped out the back door and to his car. He hadn't used his Garmin GPS in quite a while, but somehow remembered how to program in an address; 716 Colbert Dr., Fulton. The silver Camry slowly backed out of the driveway, turned, and accelerated away to the programmed destination 4.8 miles away.

He was quite familiar with the part of town that the Garmin was directing him to. There was a mall and several high-end restaurants nearby, one in particular, Keane's Steakhouse, that he and Lisa frequented at least once every other month on their date night. A quarter of a mile past the mall, the Garmin directed him off the main road and into an upscale residential development. Posey Street, then left onto Crescent. He slowly drove by a jogger and a couple of kids on bikes, as the Garmin continued to bark out directions.

The road bent slightly to the right and just as the Garmin commanded a left turn at an upcoming intersection, Ryan saw the sign for Colbert Drive. He strained to read the house number off the first mailbox he passed – 942. He was close. He continued slowly, watching the numbers decrease into the 700s. The even numbered houses were on the driver's side of the street; 722, 720, 718...716. The Camry pulled over to the curb and crawled to a stop across the street from the driveway at 716 Colbert Dr., and Ryan rolled down his window and just stared. Gawking was more like it.

The driveway, the large oak tree, the manicured lawn, the wide garage entrance on the right side of the house; it wasn't just similar to what he had dreamed, it was *exactly* as he had dreamed. His eyes were fixated on the house and the entire property, and he never noticed someone approaching.

"Do you need help with something?" The voice was deep and not in the friendliest of tones.

"Uh, no, I'm sorry. I was–"

Before he could continue, the figure looming outside his car door asked, "Are you a reporter, a cop, a friend of the Sears family?"

Ryan realized that this must have looked awfully suspicious – a stranger slowly drives up the block, stops across from a house that just days earlier had a child snatched from the driveway, and now can't explain why he's there. "No, I'm not a reporter or a cop. I don't know the Sears family but read about what happened. Listen, I have two sons of my own and have lived here in Fulton for almost 14 years. My wife and I are sick over what happened. I just happened to be nearby, that's all."

The stranger's face softened. "I'm Eddie Moore; I live next door to the Sears. You have to understand, bud, we're all just a little bit on edge right now."

"I totally understand, and again, I'm sorry. The last thing you need are strangers driving up and down the block." And with that, Ryan put the car in gear and slowly pulled away. It was all becoming very real.

# Chapter 7

That afternoon, the Fulton Police paid a visit to the Sears' home. It had been a few days since the abduction, and they were hoping that perhaps a few more details could be obtained from talking to the parents. At this point, no one had been ruled out, not even the parents. One of the officers, Greg Lenox, happened to live several blocks away with two young children of his own, so he not only empathized with Sears, but also had a personal interest in the safety of the neighborhood.

Jack and Loretta Sears already had been separately interrogated. Today was nothing more than a follow-up to see if, when asked the same questions as before, their answers were consistent; and whether they might have remembered anything new that might help the investigation.

"Mr. Sears, can you just tell me again where you were on the morning of October 16th?"

"I was at my office at Capitol Insurance in downtown Raleigh," Jack firmly answered. "I got there at 7:45 and was in my office right up until I received a call from my wife around 11 o'clock. Then I hurried home."

Officer Lenox glanced down at his notes and noted it was consistent with what he and Jack's co-workers had previously said.

"Mrs. Sears, is there anything else you can tell me about that morning? You said that you were in the garage, and your daughter was playing in the driveway, is that correct?"

Loretta Sears' face stiffened. She didn't like the way the question was put to her. "No, I was not *in* the garage, I was at the entrance of the garage, and my daughter was in full view at all times," she replied firmly.

Officer Lenox noted that she was slightly agitated in her response but continued with the questions. "So, when was the first moment you realized your daughter was missing?"

Loretta Sears inhaled deeply, clearly upset with having to answer this question yet again. "Jenny was just a few feet away from me pulling her wagon. I was sitting in a folding chair in the garage where it opens to the driveway, working on Halloween decorations. The baby was inside taking her nap, which she normally does from 10 o'clock to around noon." Loretta was wringing her hands. "I could hear Katie, that's my 8-month-old, crying inside. I did not expect her to be awake yet, and her crying didn't seem normal. My thought was to run inside and check on her, get her out of her crib, and bring her out with me. I ran inside, picked Katie up and saw that her diaper was dry, yet she was still crying. I quickly wrapped a blanket around her and hurried back out to the garage. That is when I noticed Jenny was gone." Loretta's eyes filled with tears, as she stared down at the floor, her voice tailing off to a whisper.

Officer Lenox again glanced at his notes and, again, they reflected exactly what she had said when first interviewed. "I'm sorry," Officer Lenox said. He saw the pain in both of them and didn't see the need to pursue it further. "Sometimes new information emerges from our memories after a little time passes by. If anything else comes to mind, please give us a call." With that, Officer Lenox stood and walked to the door, fully aware that the longer their girl was missing, the less likely they were to get her back.

Officer Lenox strolled slowly down the driveway back to his cruiser. He opened the driver's side door, but before getting in, took a long look back at the garage entrance and the yard on both sides of the driveway. He had a few more stops to make.

Colbert Drive intersects with Crescent Street, and at that intersection are two businesses: a Mobil gas station and a Quik-Mart convenience store. In the first few days after the abduction, a young cop and his rookie partner paid a visit to these businesses and asked the routine questions, gathered their notes, and reported back at the station to report their findings. What they failed to ask, however, was whether they had any surveillance cameras on the premises.

Even if there were, there's no guarantee that they were operational on the day of the abduction.

Officer Lenox drove to the Mobil station where he clearly observed several security cameras set up to monitor the outside area. The gas station was located on the other side of Crescent Street from where the Sears lived on Colbert Drive. He also noticed that all the cameras faced away from the intersection, focusing primarily on the gas pumps.

The name *Ted* was stitched above the Mobil logo on the shirt of the man standing behind the cash register.

"Yes sir, how can I help you?" he said with a smile as Officer Lenox entered.

"My name's Officer Lenox with the Fulton Police Department. We're investigating a crime that occurred in this area in the past week, and I was wondering if I could get a look at the video recordings from your security cameras assuming, of course, that they are in working order."

"I'll have to give my manager a call to get you that. I've never played around with the security equipment, and he's the one who takes care of the system whenever there's a problem." Ted pulled out his cell phone and promptly dialed the number. After briefly describing the situation to his manager, he let Officer Lenox know that his manager was on his way and should be there within ten minutes. Ted looked over at the officer gazing out the wide window facing the gas pumps. "Can I get you some coffee while you wait?"

"No thanks," the officer replied, as he walked back outside to get a better look at the lone camera facing the intersection. A dark green pick-up truck pulled into the Mobil parking lot and parked alongside the building. Out jumped Lee Burwell wearing his worn jeans, flannel shirt and sporting a full head of gray hair.

"You must be Officer Lenox? Lee Burwell, manager and co-owner. I understand you want to look at some video from our security system?"

"Yes sir, I do. A little girl was abducted down the block, and we're checking all the security cameras in the area."

Lee Burwell led Officer Lenox to the office at the back of the store. "I heard about that. Hope you catch that son-of-a bitch. If that was my little girl and I caught him– there wouldn't be enough of him left to fill a shoebox!" When they were in the office, Burwell went over and unlocked a closet where all the video equipment was contained. "What timeframe are you interested in?"

"October 16 beginning at around 9 a.m. until noon." The 911 call from Loretta Sears was received at 10:47 a.m. Officer Lenox wanted to see if there was anything out of the ordinary before and after that time.

It took nearly two hours to play back the requested time frame from the three outside cameras, fast forwarding through the tapes and stopping only when a vehicle or person came into view. There wasn't much activity between the hours of 9 a.m. and noon. Officer Lenox noted the time and description of each vehicle that stopped for gas as well as every individual entering the store. He didn't see anything out of the ordinary.

"Thank you for your time and cooperation, Mr. Burwell," Officer Lenox said, as he pulled on the office door to leave. The Quik-Mart across the street was his next stop

The Quik-Mart grocery store was an older business that had been operating in Fulton before many of the homes on Colbert Drive were built. The lines in the parking lot had faded over the years, replaced by patched potholes of varying sizes. Clearly whoever owned this business was not getting rich off it. As with the Mobil station, the Quik-Mart had external security cameras that covered the front and side doors. Officer Lenox entered the store and was warmly received by a man who appeared to be in his mid-sixties.

Lester Payne's family has owned and operated the Quik-Mart for the past fifty years, long before the housing boom tripled the size of Fulton. He watched as the police cruiser pulled into the lot and parked off to the side. "Good afternoon officer," Lester said as Officer Lenox entered the store.

"Good afternoon. My name's Officer Lenox and I was wondering if your security cameras outside are working."

"Why, I sure hope so! We've only had them for a year or so, and they were working the last time I checked. Anything specific you're looking for?"

"A little girl was abducted this past week from a nearby neighborhood and I'm checking all the security cameras in the area to see if anything stands out. I'd appreciate if I could view your recordings on the sixteenth of October between 9 a.m. and noon."

"Whatever I can do to help, officer," Lester said, as he motioned Lenox to follow him toward the back of the store. He had to move a stack of empty cardboard boxes to reveal cluttered shelves containing the video recording system. A nest of wiring led from the shelves to a nearby desk and monitor.

"There should be thirty days of storage from our cameras on there," Lester beamed, as he turned on the monitor and brought up the application for playing back recorded video. He then brought over a folding chair for the officer. "If you need any help–"

"Thanks, I think I can handle it from here," the officer replied.

There were two camera views, but Officer Lenox quickly dismissed the one covering the side door because it was angled straight down and provided a view only of the door and the concrete slab in front of it. The second camera was mounted under the eave at the corner of the building and provided a view of the front door, as well as a clear view of the intersection of Colbert Drive and Crescent Street.

Officer Lenox selected the camera that captured a view of the intersection, input the desired timeframe for October 16, and began playing back the video at double speed to get through it quicker, slowing it only when something appeared in view. He noted times and descriptions of everyone who entered the store as well as every vehicle seen entering and leaving the parking lot, as well as every vehicle that drove through the intersection, to and from Colbert Drive. Officer Lenox glanced at his notepad and saw that Loretta Sears had made the 911 call at 10:47 a.m. He sat up and sharpened his focus on the video when it hit the 10:30 a.m. mark.

Three vehicles were observed coming from Colbert Drive in that timeframe. At 10:33 a.m., a white BMW with what appeared to be a woman behind the wheel turned left from Colbert onto Crescent. The second vehicle, a light blue Honda Accord, arrived at the intersection at 10:37 a.m. When it stopped at the stop sign, the head of a large dog could be seen hanging out the back window before it slowly pulled away. Then, at 10:43, an old white van approached Crescent Street and turned right, making no attempt to slow down at the stop sign. There appeared to be a male driving the vehicle, but no other details were possible. Several other vehicles were noted; however, they were all observed after 11:15, nearly half an hour after the abduction was reported to have occurred.

"Thank you for your help," Lennox told Lester as exiting the store. Sitting in his patrol car, he called in to Dispatch to advise that he had completed reviewing surveillance videos and was on his way back to the station. The other officer on the case, Officer Baines, had the task of following up with neighbors of the Sears family. The plan was for them to meet back at the station and review their findings.

# Chapter 8

Driving home, Ryan was in a stupor, thinking about what he'd just seen on Colbert Drive. Every detail of the home, driveway, and yard aligned exactly with what was in his dream. But he had seen so much more in his dream – the abduction, the suspect, and the vehicle. *Strange coincidence?*

The windows were lowered to allow the rush of cool autumn air to circulate throughout the car, needed to keep Ryan focused on his drive home. Once he turned onto his street, his thoughts shifted back to his dream. *Now what?* He hadn't yet mentioned a word of this to Lisa and knows he must somehow tell her about it without sounding like a lunatic. The Camry pulled into the driveway and crept to a stop several feet in front of the garage door.

"Well, *you* were out early this morning," Lisa said, as he entered through the side door to the kitchen.

"Uh, yeah, I was planning on getting some shelving at Home Depot but didn't see what I was looking for." Ryan hated himself for the little white lie he just told, however, he just couldn't handle having the conversation at that moment.

Lisa didn't pursue it any further.

Ryan had a lost look on his face. "I don't know, just not feeling myself right now. I'm gonna lie down for a bit." Without so much as a glance at the pile of fresh-baked muffins, Ryan walked straight to the bedroom and shut the door. He sat on the edge of the bed, removed his shoes, and leaned back until his head hit the pillow. His breathing was deep and methodical as he stared up at the ceiling, picturing in his mind what he had seen earlier. He rested his arms on his chest, closed his eyes, and drifted off to sleep.

*Ryan again finds himself standing on the grass just a few feet from the driveway on Colbert Drive. Young Jennifer Sears is pulling her wagon up and down the driveway. Mom is seated by the garage entrance working on decorations and turns her head sharply toward the door leading into the house. She hesitates slightly, but then hurries into the house. And then, as if on cue, the white van rolls to a stop at the end of the driveway.*

A loud whirling noise interrupted the scene. It persisted until Ryan opens his eyes and sees the maroon drapes of his bedroom. Outside, his son Jason is wrestling with the leaf blower and the huge piles of leaves that have been neglected for the past two weekends. Ryan rubs his eyes and sits up in bed. He can't keep this in any longer.

"Are you okay?" Lisa asked, as she stopped at the doorway.

Ryan didn't answer right away, rubbing his eyes and looking confused. He is never one to take a nap on a Saturday, and she suspects he might be coming down with something. Regardless of what it is, she can clearly see that he doesn't look well. Ryan looks up and measures his words carefully.

"Hon, can you try to find that newspaper that contained the article about the abduction of the little girl?"

Lisa wasn't expecting that but left the room and returned moments later with the paper in hand.

"Can you read that story to me – slowly," Ryan said, though he knew far more details than what was stated in the article.

She could see the serious look on his face and decided this was no time for joking or her often-used sarcasm. As she read the article, Ryan just sat and nodded until she finished.

"Lisa, we have to have a talk."

# Chapter 9

After Ryan sat down with Lisa and poured out everything he could remember, her first impulse was to ask if he really was convinced of what was happening.

"So, you're telling me that you drove to the address of that home, and it was exactly what you saw in your dream?" she asked.

"Yes, that's exactly what I'm saying. But there's more. When I came home and fell back asleep earlier today, the whole scene came back again, only this time the little girl, the mom, and the white van were there as well." Ryan could tell by the pained look on Lisa's face that she was struggling with it.

"Ryan," she said softly, "let's say that everything you saw really happened. And you had this information that the police didn't have." She paused for a moment. "What if that was *our* child?" She let the words sink in. He knew exactly what she was getting at.

"Lisa, if I walk into the police station and tell them what I've told you, what happens then? Don't you think they'll be just a little curious how I know so much? Or, maybe they'll assume that I witnessed the abduction. They might even think that I was somehow involved and now feeling guilty enough to come forward." He just shook his head.

She thought for a second. "Why not an anonymous tip? Figure something out, Ryan. Please!"

He knew she was right but also knew that calls to the police station are probably recorded and could be traced. "All right, I have an idea. I'll be back in about a half-hour. Remember, please, don't say a word to anyone, especially the kids."

He grabbed a bottle of water from the refrigerator and was out the door. Ryan had heard of *burner phones* but never had a reason to ever get one. He also thought it would be better to make his calls from any town other than Fulton and knew of a Walmart on the highway toward the town of Cary.

The drive there was consumed by thoughts of what he was going to say. He knew they'd try to keep him on the phone, press him for details, and ask his identity. He needed to write down exactly what he would say, say it, and hang up.

Ryan pulled his Camry into the Walmart parking lot and tried his best to calm his nerves, as he walked in and headed to the electronics department. He wasn't exactly sure where the burner phones were located or exactly what to get, so he sought out the first employee he could find.

A middle-aged employee sporting Walmart's blue and yellow vest was just finishing up with a customer and walking his way. "Excuse me, can you help me with something? I'm heading out on a camping trip and looking for one of those disposable cell phones. I think they call it a burner phone?" Ryan hadn't been camping since he was in the Boy Scouts, but he thought it sounded plausible.

"Oh sure, right over here." He led him to a locked display case. "Any particular one you had in mind? I take the family camping quite a bit, we love it. Where you heading?" The question was innocent enough, but Ryan wasn't prepared to carry on a conversation and had to think of something quick.

"We're not sure yet, still looking at a few places near Ashville." He hoped that would satisfy the question and could just get the phone and get out of there.

Thankfully, the employee redirected the conversation back to the phone. "Well, if you just need it for a short time camping, I've got a couple of cheap, prepaid phones right here that should do the job."

Ryan pretended to think about it and, after a few seconds, simply pointed to one. He couldn't get out of the store fast enough. The Walmart shared a huge parking lot with an adjoining strip mall of small businesses and restaurants. Driving to the far end of the lot, he parked and reached into the glove compartment, pulling out an old envelope and a pen. I've got to keep this short, he thought. *Say only the key words and hang up.*

He searched on his phone for the Fulton Police Department phone number. Holding the envelope with his talking points in one hand, his other hand punched in the numbers on the burner phone, and he took a deep breath.

# Chapter 10

Despite being surrounded by shops, a pizzeria, and a few attorney offices, the Fulton Police Department easily stood out as the most recognizable building on the block. Wide glass double doors seemed to invite anyone who walked by to give a glance. Upon entering, you would find yourself restricted within a small lobby lined with several benches, a few chairs, a banister separating the lobby from a hallway that led to the back of the precinct, and a huge elevated wooden counter located front and center, behind which sat the officer in charge of greeting every visitor who walked through the door. Behind this officer and up against the window sat Sarah Bunning at her dispatch desk.

Calls come in throughout the day, and Sarah's routine is to greet the caller, note the time of the call, and get as much information as possible before rerouting the call to an officer. The phone rang, and she noted the time; 3:25 p.m. There is no caller ID for the incoming call, just a local number. The number and the conversation are automatically recorded.

"Fulton Police, may I help you?" she says in a flat yet friendly tone. The male voice on the other end sounds calm. "Jennifer Sears, abduction, white van, white male 25-30 years of age, slender, roughly six foot tall, North Carolina license plate RZN 1110." *Click.*

The call was over in a matter of seconds, not enough time for Sarah to get a word in. She was, however, able to scribble down the key words from the call and write down the phone number that appeared on her screen. The caller provided very specific information about a crime that had just occurred in Fulton, a crime with no leads. The day had suddenly taken on a new complexion. Getting up from her desk, she looked over at Officer Riley Ortman, who was seated up high behind the reception counter. "Riley, can you handle the phones for a few minutes? This is important; I've got to speak with Sgt. Ramos for a second."

Ramos was back in his office with the door slightly ajar, presiding over a desk cluttered with folders, a few framed pictures, an old coffee cup, an oversized nameplate, and around a dozen small trinkets given to him over the years. When asked, he could recite the story behind every article on his desk, whether it was the status of a case, the donor of a trinket, or the event of where a picture had been taken. In his hands was the folder of Jennifer Sears.

# Chapter 11

Sgt. Joe Ramos leaned back in his chair casting a blank look at the Jennifer Sears file in his hand. The case had investigators from the Fulton Police Department, the county sheriff's department, and the state's Bureau of Investigation, however, communication between the three of them was minimal at best. Ramos found himself having to initiate the calls and relay information about the case between the three agencies. He leaned forward, placed the file down, and rubbed his brow, as he peered over at the scribbled notes written on his whiteboard. No clues, no suspects, no witnesses.

A rapid knock on the door disturbed his train of thought. Without waiting for an invitation, Sarah pushed the door open and marched right in.

"Sarge, you're going to want to hear this! Just got a call with information about the Jennifer Sears abduction."

Ramos sat up straight and eyes grew wide.

"And before you ask, the caller wouldn't identify himself, there was no caller ID, and we were unable to get a trace on it." She then handed him the notes she had scribbled during the call.

"This sounds like someone who witnessed the whole thing. Probably a neighbor. Or it's some moron playing a sick joke, which is why he didn't identify himself. Or it could be the kidnapper himself playing with us. I want to listen to the tape."

Sarah Bunning, the only non-police employee at the department, had been managing the day-to-day operations there for nearly 25 years, and was adept at handling the recording equipment located in the conference room. She queued up the tape and left the room, leaving Sgt. Ramos to himself.

*The voice was calm.* He continued to listen intently to the vocabulary used, pronunciation of the words, and whether he could detect any sort of accent. *He's not young, but he's not old,* Ramos thought. He scribbled down *30-45 years-old, most likely Caucasian.* He did not speak in full sentences, only precise details in the fewest words possible. *He obviously was considering time as a factor and not wanting to be traced.* The number that came up on the caller ID panel was useless, a random burner phone number. *This was not a spur of the moment call; it was planned.*

Sgt. Ramos headed to his office to add the notes taken from this call to his whiteboard and file on his desk. Outside, Officers Lenox and Baines were returning in their separate patrol cars from the interviews they performed from the Colbert Drive residents and nearby businesses. Before they could settle down at their desks, Sgt. Ramos shouted out to them, "Baines, Lenox, can you come in here please?"

The officers, notepads in hand, entered the office, neither choosing to sit down. Officer Baines spoke first. "Nothing new from any of the neighbors. I was able to speak with the one family that we hadn't received a statement from before, but they said that they were away for the past ten days so naturally, they had nothing to offer."

Sgt. Ramos shifted his attention to Officer Lenox, who glanced down at his notes before speaking. "No new details from Mr. and Mrs. Sears; their stories are consistent with the original statement they gave. I did, however, visit a gas station and convenience store at the end of Colbert Drive, both of which had working security cameras. The cameras at the gas station focused mainly on the pumps and the front door. But across the street was another story. One camera outside used for viewing the front door also provided a good view of the corner of Colbert and Crescent, which provided more of a look at vehicle traffic. The manager allowed me access to his recorded video, so I focused on the timeframe between the hours of 10 a.m. and noon on the 16th." Lenox handed a sheet of paper to Sgt. Ramos. "Here are the times and descriptions of everyone who entered the Quik-Mart, as well as all the vehicles that passed through that intersection."

Sgt. Ramos scanned the list, and then his eyes froze. There it was, at 10:43 a.m. – a white van approached from the right, meaning it was on Colbert Drive coming from the direction of the Sears home. Ramos took note of a comment Lenox wrote in the right-hand margin of the page which read: *white van sped through stop sign, turned right onto Crescent Street*.

The recorded call that Sgt. Ramos had listened to mentioned a white van and a lot more. He looked up at his white board and saw that the 911 call came in at 10:45 a.m. This *had* to be it.

# Chapter 12

"We received a call today from an unidentified caller providing us with random bits of information that appear to be connected to the Sears abduction this past week. The caller specifically used the words *abduction, white male, and white van*." Sgt. Ramos paused while Officers Lenox and Baines stood silent. "He also provided a description of the suspect and a license plate number. Like I said, the caller would not identify himself and hung up before we could engage with him. And the only information that came up on our screen was a local phone number – which proved useless because it was from one of those disposable burners."

Sgt. Ramos took a deep breath and exhaled slowly. "It's all we got right now, and time is critical. I need one of you to run the records on that license plate and let me know what you find. Let's go!"

Officers Baines and Lenox turned to leave when Sarah appeared at the doorway holding a sheet of paper. "Here's the info on that white van. *A 1994 white Dodge Grand Caravan, North Carolina license plate RZN1110*. Records show that it belongs to Darrell Jacob Pickens, 420 Shadetree Drive, Clayton, NC."

"Thanks Sarah. I'm heading over to see Judge Hastings and get a warrant. Notify Sheriff Wickham and the folks at the Bureau of Investigation. Tell them we're on our way there now. Baines, Lenox, you two head over there. I shouldn't be far behind."

Sgt. Ramos called the judge and filled him in on why he needed the warrant. It was waiting for him when he got to the courthouse. With blue lights flashing, his cruiser sped out of town as vehicles in his path peeled off to the side of the road. Normally a twenty-minute drive, he planned to make it there in ten as the late afternoon sun crept toward the horizon. If there was indeed something to find in predominantly rural Clayton, doing it while still light outside was a must. Ramos caught up with Baines and Lenox and the three-car convoy cruised through the backroads until they reached the Clayton town limits.

Sgt. Ramos, driving the lead car, reached for his radio. "Dispatch, this is Sgt. Ramos. Sarah, you there?"

Sarah had glued herself to the dispatch desk the moment they left the station house. "This is Dispatch, go ahead Joe."

The Fulton convoy found themselves on a narrow, paved road after they drove through the one main road that passed through the business district of Clayton.

"Sarah, I forgot to ask you to contact the Clayton PD and let them know we're coming in."

"Already took care of it. Police Chief Ballo of the Clayton PD will be waiting for you at the foot of Shadetree Drive."

"Copy that, Sarah. We should be there any minute."

He glanced at the GPS and saw that Shadetree Drive was just around the bend up ahead. With Lenox and Baines trailing right behind, he slowed around the curve and there, parked on the gravel were two Clayton patrol cars. The three from Fulton pulled in behind them. On cue, everyone got out of their cars and came together near the front car.

"Chief Ballo? I'm Sgt. Ramos, Fulton PD. I understand that my dispatch has filled you in?" Sgt. Ramos didn't want to waste a lot of time with formalities.

Chief Anthony Ballo didn't care much for formalities either. "This fella, DJ Pickens...he's no stranger to us. We've had issues with his family for years and he's been in and out of trouble most of his life. Haven't heard much of him recently, though."

Sgt. Ramos interjected, "We received a tip about a young girl who was kidnapped earlier this week in Fulton. His vehicle was mentioned as being in the area at the time and we'd like to have a word with him."

"Well, he lives up the road about a quarter mile. The house is back a ways off the road. There's a gravel road up ahead here that takes you around to the back of his property. My deputy can lead your men there and we can approach from the front."

Ramos nodded and looked over to the other Fulton officers. "Len-ox, you and Baines follow the deputy."

The five-car convoy quietly headed out, with the Clayton deputy splitting off, followed by Lenox and Baines. Sgt. Ramos and Chief Ballo continued up the rural road and pulled off to the side just prior to reaching the house. Ramos could see the small one-story brick home with a long dirt and gravel driveway leading to the back of the property. Alongside the house was a white Dodge van. A few large trees scattered on the property towered over a yard desperately in need of attention. The sun, just minutes from disappearing, was at their back and the shades were drawn down on all the windows. Ballo made his way to the side of the house while Ramos approached the front door, hand hovering over his holster.

Just as he lightly tapped on the door, he noticed an ever so slight movement of the window shade. A second, harder knock at the door was followed by the sounds of someone inside running. Identifying himself, Sgt. Ramos then lunged forward and threw his shoulder into the door, stumbling into the living room as the wood around the door jamb splintered. He could hear the frantic footsteps of DJ Pickens sprinting through the kitchen and out the back door. Sgt. Ramos ran to the back door to see that Mr. Pickens was locked in a bear hug by Officer Baines. Pickens, who probably weighed around 150 pounds was no match for the officer who was known for his football days back in high school and as a regular at the Fulton fitness center.

Sgt. Ramos turned to search the home. "Anyone in here? Hello?" he repeatedly shouted, as he went from room to room. Nothing upstairs, but he thought he heard movements coming from the basement. He approached the door with gun drawn, turned on the light and slowly descended the stairs into a large, musty room cluttered with boxes, a stack of rotted wood, and an old card table and chairs. His eyes scanned the room when again he heard a faint noise coming from behind a door further back in the basement. The door was locked from the outside with a deadbolt. Gun in hand, he quietly approached the door and unlocked the deadbolt. In one furious move, he threw open the door and let out a gasp.

Out back, DJ Pickens was lying face down on the floor. "I didn't hurt her! I was never going to hurt her," DJ shouted, shouted at the officers pinning him down. Meanwhile, three-year-old Jennifer Sears, hair disheveled and dressed in dirty clothes, was found on the floor in the back room of the basement holding an old doll and playing with a few dirty toys.

# Chapter 13

Ryan wore a lost look on his face, as he took his place at the head of the table. He wasn't in much of a mood to eat and just picked at the food on his plate. There wasn't the usual laughter at dumb jokes or banter about what the kids were up to that day, just the sounds of forks scraping plates. A glance at the clock; it was almost six. He shoveled the remaining few pieces of meatloaf into his mouth and excused himself from the table and bolted to the family room. Jason and Aaron could be heard begging for dessert as Lisa cleared the table.

Ryan eased into his favorite recliner and reached for the remote. Jason, clutching a few cookies, threw himself onto the couch nearby. "Dad, I think *Forrest Gump* is on soon."

Ryan put his hand up as if to stop Jason in his tracks. The local news was about to begin, and he was anxious to see if there was any mention of an anonymous call to the police today. He got his answer in the first few seconds of the broadcast. "*Breaking news tonight, kidnapped girl found alive!*"

Lisa heard this from the kitchen and rushed right in. "Oh, thank God!" Ryan and Lisa just looked at each other but said nothing as the newscaster described the details provided by the Fulton police chief. "*Twenty-eight-year-old DJ Pickens of Clayton was taken into custody late this afternoon. Police also recovered the white van they believed was used in the abduction.*"

The Clayton police chief was in front of the microphone speaking to a crowd of reporters on the scene, accompanied by several other law officers. A reporter asked, "What break did you get in the case that led you to the suspect?"

Police Chief Ballo simply stated that an anonymous tip had been received by the Fulton Police Department. "At this time, we just want to report that three-year-old Jennifer Sears has been found and appears to be unharmed and in good health. The suspect has confessed and been taken into custody."

Jason could see that his parents were seriously glued to the news, and decided it was better to just watch his movie upstairs with his brother. They didn't even notice him leave the room.

Ryan turned to look up at Lisa standing nearby. "Do you realize what's happened here?" she said in a barely audible voice. She rested her hand on his shoulder. "Oh my God, Ryan! Because of *you*, that little girl is safe and will be back home with her family!"

Ryan nodded but was a million miles away in his thoughts. The enormity of what just happened was overwhelming. He was able to provide information that no one else could provide. He was able to witness the event not once, but *repeatedly*. He leaned back in the recliner but didn't want to close his eyes. Not this time.

Immediately after the child was found, there was speculation from reporters, investigators, and interested members of the community that whoever provided this anonymous tip must be someone who either witnessed the abduction firsthand or knew the suspect personally.

The authorities and media began focusing on the anonymous tip. Why was the person who supplied the tip afraid to go public? Regardless, Sgt. Joe Ramos, the Sears family, and the entire Fulton com-munity was overwhelmed with joy and relief, and hopeful for a return to normalcy. Ryan and Lisa Field knew that what was happening was anything but normal.

# Chapter 14

Raleigh, a city of less than half a million people, has small town charm yet provides everything you'd want from a large city – a professional hockey team, a bustling downtown of businesses and restaurants, and a major university. It is also in close proximity to Raleigh-Durham Airport, two other major universities (Duke and University of North Carolina), and the Research Triangle Park. The FBI office in Raleigh is a popular choice for agents seeking an assignment. Aside from the desirable quality of life, it was comfortably located far enough away from Washington's political influence.

Agent Mike McShea knew he had made the right decision the moment he drove across the state line from Virginia into North Carolina. The closer he got to Raleigh, the more excited he became. He grew up in a law enforcement family; his father was a career analyst for the FBI, his older brother was a cop in New Jersey, and his mother wrote software programs for multiple government agencies.

During high school, Mike always seemed to do just enough to get by, and if he had one strength, it was always being able to identify where the short cuts were. After receiving his degree in data analytics from the University of Richmond and with some help from his dad, he applied to and was accepted at the FBI academy.

For twelve years, Agent Mike McShea worked out of the Washington office, but had grown tired of the scenery and needed a change. He was single and mobile and had invested many hours researching the FBI field offices in the country for his next assignment. The choice came down to Miami or Raleigh. He understood that the field office in Miami was a pressure cooker, dealing with non-stop immigration and drug issues. Raleigh appeared to be a bit quieter and more laid back. Agent Mike

McShea was anxious to remove himself from the hyperactive chaos that Washington had been and blend into the background in a more subdued environment. When an opening in the Raleigh office became available, he jumped on it.

In those first two years at his new field office, Agent Mike McShea handled what he considered "routine cases" but kept a low profile at work and in his private life. He was relieved to have escaped the Washington politics that always seemed to find its way into many of the cases he had worked before. He was still to some degree, a loner who lived in a two-bedroom apartment on the north side of Raleigh. Occasionally, he joined other agents out for a beer on Friday nights, but his passion was being near the water, and he often made the two-hour drive to Wrightsville Beach or the Outer Banks. His dream had always been to live near the water, own a large boat, and spend his retirement fishing and cruising the Caribbean. He hoped that the relocation to North Carolina would be one step closer to that dream.

# Chapter 15

One week had passed since Ryan and Lisa watched the evening newscast about Jennifer Sears and the apprehension of DJ Pickens. Although the crime was solved, Sgt. Joe Ramos kept its file on the corner of his desk as well as all the details on the white board. His mind would drift back to that phone call with the anonymous tip. *Why did the caller make such an effort not to be identified? He described the vehicle in detail and a description of the abductor but did not provide Pickens' name. That might mean that he didn't know who it was, but he certainly knew the vehicle...which meant that he had to have been there when it happened.*

As Sgt. Ramos labored over the details of the solved abduction, Ryan returned to work at the North Carolina Transit Authority after a weekend tending to honey-dos around the house. No matter how intently he engaged in his work, nagging thoughts of the past week interfered. He was studying a blueprint stretched across his desk when the office door pushed open.

"Ryan!" Joe Farrell seemed to have startled him. "Are you coming to the staff meeting?" Ryan looked down at his watch. Ten minutes past one.

"Damn!" he said under his breath. "Sorry, I lost track of time." He quickly grabbed his notebook and followed Joe out the door.

As they hurried down the narrow hall, Farrell, who was a long-time colleague and friend of Ryan's just had to ask what everyone there seemed to be thinking. "Hey man, everything OK? Want to head out for a beer after work?"

*OK, this is not good,* Ryan thought. *Joe's known me for a while, and he can smell bullshit a mile away.*

"Just a lot of stuff going on at home, nothing serious. And yeah, how 'bout we get out Friday night for a few beers and some wings?" They had reached the conference room, so at least for the moment, he was relieved of any further inquiries from his colleague.

Lisa was the only other person who knew what was going on, so she understood the distraction and the mood swings that plagued Ryan in the past week. The boys noticed, too, but didn't think much of it, no doubt attributing it to "grown-up problems." Lisa was still somewhat baffled by all that was happening, and she secretly wished that it would all just fade away so that Ryan wouldn't be so distracted, and they could get back to the way things were. She lowered herself into a chair at the kitchen table and could hear the boys arguing about something upstairs, not an unusual occurrence when they were playing their video game. It was 5:20, and Ryan would be home at any moment.

It seemed to be a different mood every day. What would it be today, she wondered, as the car pulled up the driveway? Just the same, she walked over to the cupboard, pulled out two wine glasses, and set them on the counter near a corked bottle of Merlot. Ryan walked through the door with that lost look on his face, one that Lisa has seen a lot of recently.

"Hey babe, how was your day?" She could see that something was weighing on him, but that didn't necessarily mean he'd talk about it. He gave her a forced smile, a kiss on the cheek, and turned to reach for the corkscrew.

"They're beginning to notice at work, at least Joe's noticing. I almost missed our staff meeting today. Probably would have if it hadn't been for him coming to get me."

Lisa looked Ryan dead in the eye. "I know this has really been weighing on you, but it's over. Maybe we'll never be able to understand or explain it, but you did a good thing and now we just need to move on from it." She waited to see the effects of her words as he drew a deep breath.

"There's more. I probably should have told you earlier, but I wanted to make sure." Hearing this, she sat down, never taking her eyes off him. Ryan stared out the window and began to speak.

"There were other dreams, two that I recently remembered, but I was caught up in the abduction of that little girl because it was right here in Fulton. You read that article to me...I drove and actually saw the house... and then, I dreamt of it again that afternoon when I came home and laid down. And no, I can't explain it!

Ryan turned and paced around the kitchen. "The two others...in one, I witnessed a young woman near a college campus being struck by a vehicle. In the other, a boy playing baseball was struck by light-ning. Neither one had anything to do with the other, but both were very real to me... and they also happened!

"One night after work, I did an internet search on the words, *woman, college campus, hit and run*. It didn't take long before I found a recent story of a 20-year-old junior at NC State who was killed in a hit and run near campus. It sounded very much like what I saw." He paused. "The little boy playing baseball...he was standing out there in the outfield. A light rain was falling and out of nowhere, a blinding bolt of lightning struck where the boy was standing. There was chaos everywhere...Anyway, I did the same thing; I researched the internet and found that a boy had recently died after being struck by lightning during a baseball game. And just like with the campus hit and run, the details provided in the article matched exactly with what I saw. I wrote down everything."

Lisa cleared her throat. She brushed back her hair with her hands. "So now what?"

Ryan took a seat at the table. "When I came home that day and laid down... I fell asleep and the whole dream about the abduction came back to me."

"Are you saying that you think you could do the same for these two dreams?"

Ryan shrugged. "Maybe."

# Chapter 16

Several days had quietly passed since Ryan and Lisa discussed those other two dreams. Ryan started keeping a low profile at work, avoided Joe Farrell as much as possible, and made an extra effort to focus on work issues and not let his mind stray. One afternoon around quitting time while he was hunched over his desk immersed in a design drawing, a tap on the door jarred his concentration.

“So, are we on for tomorrow after work?” Joe Farrell hadn’t forgotten. Without hesitation, Ryan looked up and responded, “Absolutely, been looking forward to it.” He hoped his quick, enthusiastic response was convincing. Joe seemed relieved to see his friend back to his old self.

“Sounds good. Let’s plan on the Ale House at 5.”

Driving home that night, Ryan felt more enthusiastic about his job and looked forward to getting out for a beer. After a couple of nights trying to “revisit” another one of his prior dreams without any success, he wondered if perhaps this crazy dream ability might have run its course.

The hundred-year-old oak trees that lined his street had already shed most of their leaves. The neighbor’s kids were still playing outside, and they waved as Ryan cruised by them and swung up the driveway. He sat for a moment before getting out of the car, still obsessed with the campus hit and run. He had already been able to revisit that dream once but retained few details from that visit. Ryan was bothered that the case was never solved.

“Hey dad!” yelled a voice from outside his driver side window. Ryan’s head snapped to his left to see Aaron standing by the car. He grabbed his laptop from the passenger seat and jumped out.

“Hey sport, how was your day?” Ryan said. “C’mon, let’s get inside, I’m starving!”

Lisa and the boys all noticed a happier, more relaxed Ryan arrive home that day. Laughter and family chatter had returned to the dinner table, and this was followed by some TV time in the family room. Everything appeared to be back to normal, at least from Lisa and the boys' perspective.

Around 9:30 that night, the boys took off for their rooms while Ryan and Lisa remained in the family room, discussing random topics ranging from a home being sold down the block, to the vacuum cleaner that decided to quit working earlier in the day.

"Okay, I've got a dishwasher to load," Lisa said, as she bounced up off the couch. She was elated at seeing Ryan laugh again and engage with her and the kids. He followed her into the kitchen to take out the garbage. When he returned, Lisa had already disappeared into the bedroom to take her nightly shower. Ryan heard the water running in the master bedroom, as well as the boys squabbling upstairs, so he quietly walked to his man cave and shut the door behind him.

From the upper drawer of his desk, Ryan withdrew the folder of notes he had written down from his internet search of those two scenes that appeared in his head, specifically, the notes from the campus hit and run. His eyes slowly scanned the key words...*Boylan Street...NC State campus...September 17th...7 pm...Allison Tate*. The mental picture began to appear. He suddenly realized that the house was silent and felt it was better to stop what he was doing and join his wife. He quickly read through the entire folder of the hit and run, before tossing it back in the drawer and heading to bed.

Lisa was already under the sheets with her nightstand light turned off when Ryan entered the room. He quickly undressed, used the bathroom, and quietly slipped under the covers. The digital clock read 10:15 when he leaned over, kissed Lisa good night, and switched off his light. The date, time, and location of what happened to Allison Tate was fresh on his mind as he turned onto his side, closed his eyes, and drifted off to sleep.

*The neighborhood was old, and the houses were placed closely together with tiny, manicured yards, located in the shadow of the NC State campus. Most were occupied by students or residents who had resided there their whole lives. Parked cars competed for every available curbside opportunity. The sun had already set, and the streetlights were on despite the orange glow in the sky. I stood there, leaning against one of those parked vehicles watching as a pair of distant headlights approached.*

*I saw a reflection of movement, what turned out to be a bicycle, quietly approaching from the same direction. As both descended upon me in unison, I turned to see a dog streaking between two parked cars and sprinting across the road. Instantly, the car's brakes screeched as the vehicle lurched right to avoid the dog, yet forcefully striking the bicycle and its occupant. I saw him. He just sat there...frozen. He appeared to be no more than 18. Cherry red Mustang. In just a few seconds, he put the car back in gear, turned the wheel and sped away. The dog, unharmed, was long gone and all that remained was a crumpled bike and a severely injured young woman. As the car sped away, I noted the license plate number.*

The obnoxious bleeps of the alarm clock woke both Ryan and Lisa. Ryan had immediate recollection of where he'd just been and laid wide-eyed after shutting off the disturbing alarm. Lisa stirred, rolled over to face Ryan, but before she could say good morning, the look on his face caused her to pause.

"What is it?" she asked but already knew the answer.

"I was there. I saw the hit and run of that girl on the bike, the car, the driver..." He stared into space. "Lisa, this is the second time it's happened. The second time I've gone back to the exact same dream and seen everything that's happened." He sat up on the edge of the bed. "I'm not going to the office today; there's something I need to do."

# Chapter 17

After a quick shower, Ryan dressed and met Lisa in the kitchen, where she was already pouring two cups from a fresh pot of coffee. She could see that he was breathing heavily, and his mind was all over the place. He reached into his pocket and placed the burner phone on the table.

"I can't *not* say something. I read that it's still under investigation. There were no witnesses and so far, no suspects. Lisa, I saw the car! I saw the driver!"

Ryan poured himself a bowl of cereal, placed it on the table, then began pacing around the kitchen. "I don't want to call from here." Without touching his breakfast, he walked to the table, grabbed the burner, and shoved it in his pocket. "I'll be back in a little bit."

He left his neighborhood and headed for familiar back roads out of Fulton. After driving for almost 15 minutes, he found himself back on the main road and pulled into the parking lot of a Domino's Pizza store that wouldn't be open for a few hours. Ryan backed into a parking space so that he'd be able to see any cars heading his way. He pulled out his iPhone to search for the Raleigh Police Department number. He then pulled out the burner phone and punched it in.

"Raleigh Police Department, Sgt. Oliver speaking, how may I help you?"

Ryan took a deep breath. "There was a hit and run accident on September 17$^{th}$ on Boylan Avenue near campus. A woman on a bike was hit. The vehicle was a late model red Mustang, North Carolina license plate NBT1442. Young male, dark hair." *Click.*

***

The hit and run incident near the NC State campus was still under investigation and there were no active leads. Random tips were received but none of them ever panned out, until Ryan made his anonymous call nearly two months after the incident occurred. The information provided by Ryan's call differed from the previous calls which had only suggested individuals as suspects for vague reasons. When Ryan's call was played back by investigators, they heard a confidant voice relaying specific details about a vehicle that the police could easily verify. When they did, they found that the car's license plate was for a 2018 red Ford Mustang registered to Wendell Taylor at 21 Southampton Lane, Durham, N.C.

Raleigh officer Sgt. Oliver called over to the Durham police to coordinate a visit to the home of Wendell Taylor. The Taylor home was in an upscale neighborhood with neatly trimmed lawns and lined with healthy red maple trees. The Durham police cruiser pulled up in front of the home. Walking up the front walkway, the officers could hear barking coming from inside the house, which only intensified once they knocked on the door.

Cracking the door slightly while holding her dog back, Samantha Taylor smiled and apologized on the dog's behalf.

"Good morning, ma'am. I'm Officer Keegan, and this is Officer Sachs. Is there a Wendell Taylor residing here?"

"Yes, that's my husband, but he's not here right now, he's at work."

The officers gave a look to each other. The information they had from the anonymous call was a young man. "Does he own a red Ford Mustang?"

"Oh, that's my son Zachary's car," Mrs. Taylor said. "Is there a problem?"

"Where can we find your son? We'd just like to ask him a few questions."

"He's a student at NC State. He usually gets home between 2:30 and 3." She knew her son had been in some trouble before on campus but never anything that warranted a visit by the police.

"Thank you, ma'am, we'll try back later."

Later that afternoon, the Durham Police returned to the Taylor home and immediately noticed the red Mustang parked at the back end of the driveway. Before knocking on the front door, both officers took a slow walk up the driveway to look at the vehicle.

"Take a look at this," Officer Sachs said, as he pointed to the front of the car. Officer Keegan walked over and looked down at the dented right front corner of the vehicle. Neither said a word, as they walked back down the driveway toward the front door. After putting the family dog away in a back room, Mrs. Taylor welcomed in the officers then called her son down. Zachary Taylor fidgeted on the couch and had trouble making eye contact with the officers when asked a question. Their training told them young Zachary was hiding something. Before continuing, they advised him that he would need to come down to the station for formal questioning and could bring a lawyer if it made him feel more comfortable.

Down at the station house, eighteen-year-old Zach Taylor was questioned for nearly three hours before he broke down and confessed to the accidental hit and run death of Allison Tate.

That evening, Ryan and Lisa Field watched the nightly news as it revealed what Ryan had already known regarding the tragic hit and run incident near the NC State campus. He had now saved a young child and helped to solve the death of a college student, yet despite that, Ryan still felt lost in his own head. Lisa, on the other hand, thought that if Ryan really did have this ability to "go places" in his dreams, that perhaps it could be done to save people and perform other good deeds. She would wait until the right time to discuss her thoughts with Ryan, who was still not comfortable with what he's able to do.

# Chapter 18

For the sake of his own sanity, Ryan dedicated himself to doing two things. First, upon waking up each day, he'd make a note of his night's dreams. If nothing else, he wanted to maintain a sort of journal that he would keep tucked away. Secondly, he would avoid going to bed thinking about details of any particular dream. Perhaps, he thought, this ability to revisit a dream was just temporary, and if he avoided pursuing it, it might just go away.

Lisa, though, took a different stance on all of this. She saw Ryan as having a tremendous gift that should be used for good, so she made it a daily ritual to watch the news and read internet stories, noting crimes and atrocities that appeared hopelessly unsolved. As someone who would go so far as to rescue an injured squirrel on the side of the road, it was certainly no surprise that she'd want Ryan to do whatever he could to help people in need.

Two weeks had passed since Ryan's last anonymous call, and he spoke less and less about his dreams. Lisa had compiled quite a journal of incidents, both local and statewide ranging from robberies to assaults, to home break-ins. *If Ryan really does have the ability to dream his way to the scene of a crime, imagine all the crimes and injustices he could have an impact on*, she thought.

One night after dinner, as the two were watching the news, the news anchor reported on a story of a local woman who was robbed after making a withdrawal at her bank. The heartbreaking story was made worse because she's a single mother who Lisa recognized as someone she saw often while shopping at the Wynn Dixie in town. As they were watching, Ryan looked over and could see Lisa's eyes welling up.

"I see her almost every week when I grocery shop there," Lisa said softly.

Ryan didn't have to ask. He didn't have to say anything at all. A single mom, robbed of her money, and Lisa is acquainted with her. He reached over and held her hand.

***

The next morning, Sarah Bunning was polishing off a powdered donut and large coffee, as she filled out a list of needed office supplies. Every so often the phone would ring, but it was usually just a matter of rerouting the call to another desk. Shortly after answering one call, the phone immediately rang again. The inconvenience caused her to quickly swallow the remaining piece of her donut. She finally got to it on the third ring.

"Fulton Police Department, may I help you?" Sarah almost sounded annoyed.

"Mrs. Sheri Latham was robbed leaving the Bank of America two days ago. The suspect is Caucasian, mid-forties, iron cross tattoo on the right side of his neck, drives a black Honda Accord, NC license plate BFR 8124." *Click.*

The Fulton Police Department didn't get many anonymous calls and now they had received two in the past couple of months. This one felt eerily similar to the first she received. She didn't bother calling Sgt. Ramos but instead made a beeline for his office.

"Joe, just got another anonymous call. This one's about the Latham robbery." She stood there as if she had more to say.

"And?" Sgt. Ramos knew there was more just by the look on her face.

"It reminded me of the last one we got, you know, the little girl? Same flat voice, same brief details, and then he hangs up." She now had his full attention.

"Queue it up, let's have a listen. And pull the tape from that last call." Sgt. Ramos gathered his notepad and followed her to the conference room. It was the same voice all right. But there was something else that confirmed it for him – the phone number.

Although the number was assigned to the same burner phone. Ramos wondered aloud, "So exactly why does this guy want to remain anonymous?"

Following up on the tip revealed the car and its owner. Although they were unable to recover the stolen cash, they *were* able to recover Sheri Latham's wallet and credit cards hidden under the suspect's car seat. The next morning, Sgt. Joe Ramos sat behind his desk, pleased that two crimes had now been solved with help from an anonymous source, yet perplexed as to how the two were connected. Was the caller just a good Samaritan? Perhaps he was just overthinking it. Either way, the open cases were now closed. Was it really worth delving into?

***

Over the next few days, Ryan and Lisa watched the local news and scoured the Fulton Times, however, nothing was reported about the Latham robbery. *He was there*. He knew what he had seen, and he provided everything the police needed. Why hadn't they acted on it? Ryan *needed to know whether or not they took his tip seriously*.

"Lisa, who's that officer downtown that you and the boys met while volunteering at that fundraiser a couple of years ago?" he shouted from his office.

Lisa appeared in the doorway. "I believe his name was Ramos. Why do you ask?"

Ryan was pounding a pencil on his desk. "It's been three days, and I haven't heard a damn thing regarding the information I gave them. I'm going to call, anonymously of course, and inquire about Sheri Latham, as if I'm a friend."

***

The next day, Sarah Bunning sat at her desk gazing out the

window waiting for the next lightning strike to occur. She watched people pressed together under umbrellas pass by while those without them ran through the steady downpour and jumped over puddles. The front desk phone rang, and she jumped to answer it. She thought nothing of the local number that appeared on the screen. What she did notice was that there was no name displayed.

"May I speak to Sgt. Joe Ramos, please?"

"May I have your name please before I transfer you?" Sarah didn't appear to be too alarmed.

"It's a friend." She wrote down the caller's number on a pad. Ryan was aware that they recorded calls but wasn't sure about whether they could accurately track a burner phone. Just to be safe, he wanted to keep it brief.

*A friend who doesn't want to leave their name?*

Sarah had worked long enough in this office and answered too many calls to know when something isn't quite right. She remained calm and put the call through. "One moment, please."

"This is Sgt. Ramos."

"Sgt. Ramos, can you tell me if they found the person who robbed Mrs. Latham?"

Ramos was silent for a moment. He looked up as Sarah rushed into his office and set down a piece of paper with the phone number of the caller. Sgt. Ramos looked over at his white board and recognized the number immediately. "Yes, that case has been solved. Thank you for the tip."

*Click.* The line went dead.

# Chapter 19

Two years earlier, Lisa and her sons Jason and Aaron had volunteered at the annual fundraising festival downtown. Sgt. Ramos and some of his trainees at the precinct were providing security at the family-friendly event and thought nothing of giving some of the young volunteers rides in their 4-wheelers. The Fulton Police, and Sgt. Ramos in particular, were easily recognizable figures in the small community and all well-liked by the residents. Sgt. Joe Ramos was considered by most as one of the friendliest, more dependable officers in the town. Last year, Lisa got sick and had to leave the festival early. The boys pleaded with her to allow them to stay if they could get a ride home. Sgt. Ramos gladly volunteered to drive the boys home at the end of the day.

***

Lisa had begun to secretly compile notes and cut out articles of local crimes. She had even started keeping tabs on sensational, unsolved crimes outside of Fulton, even outside of North Carolina. If it was up to her, she'd solve every one of them. But for now, she would love nothing more than to help her local law enforcement and her community. It broke her heart to hear about local businesses getting robbed, homes of seniors being broken into, or women being assaulted, especially if the crime had gone unsolved. The fact that Ryan seemed to want "his newfound ability" to go away didn't help.

Nearly a week passed since his conversation with Sgt. Ramos, and Ryan did all he could to keep a low profile, driving straight to work, then straight home. He did his best to avoid discussions with Lisa by finding projects around the house that needed to be completed, many of them requiring him to work in the garage or outdoors. Family discussion at the dinner table began tapering off and watching the evening news with Lisa had become awkward. Ryan knew that every time a crime was reported on the news, he'd feel those sympathetic eyes all over him, as if pleading to intervene.

Over the winter months, Ryan would experience the occasional horrific dream, witnessing a situation where something goes terribly wrong. Upon waking the following morning, he would find himself having to either fight the urge to follow up on it or live with the guilt of doing nothing. Lisa learned to back off a little from asking Ryan to intervene unless it involved a missing child or some other heinous crime where the police had no leads. Ryan would agree and of course, the calls made were still "anonymous," but always routed to one specific person in the Fulton PD.

Sgt. Joe Ramos still didn't know the identity of the caller, but he was pretty sure that he was a local and meant no ill will. All anonymous tips were being routed through Sgt. Ramos and he became known for notifying authorities in other jurisdictions with information leading to solving their crimes. He still doesn't know why he was the one chosen for this role, but there appeared to be no harm in it. Besides, crimes were being solved. At least for now.

# Chapter 20

One Saturday night, while Jason and Aaron were long into a video war game battle, their parents sat quietly in the dimly lit family room nursing a glass of their favorite Merlot. Ryan had been feeling somewhat disengaged at work lately and was not much better at home. He felt it was time to talk. He asked Lisa to shut off the TV.

"Lisa, I know I'm haven't handled this really well. Yeah, there's been some good that's come from it, I won't deny that." He paused before continuing. "I feel like I've drifted away from the boys, from you, and certainly from my work."

"Hon, stop beating yourself up. You didn't ask for this. And who knows, it may go away as fast as it came. But think for a moment the good that you've done, and what you're capable of doing." She gripped his hand and looked deep into his eyes. "If you're really able to put yourself at a certain place at a certain time, do you even have the slightest idea of what that means?"

Ryan had wanted to downplay and diminish what he's been capable of while Lisa was hinting at taking this in another direction. He was quick to respond. "You do know that this can't get out. I mean, think about *that*. If it was known that there's someone out there who could find people who have gone missing, solve unsolved crimes, or basically be an eyewitness to something that previously didn't have one, what do you think the response to that would be?"

She took a sip of wine and looked off into space. "Chaos. Maddening chaos."

Ryan's words flew out. "Exactly! No one would believe it. The only rational response would be that this person would somehow have to have been involved, know who's involved, or was an eyewitness. I've been trying so hard to hide behind the curtain, but now I'm thinking that I may have screwed up by using the burner phone!"

Lisa had a puzzled look on her face. "I thought those phones couldn't be traced to a person?"

"Lisa, I've used the *same* phone each time I called in a tip! If they compare the number of each anonymous call..."

Lisa never really understood burner phones. "So why haven't they been able to identify you?"

Ryan shrugged. "Maybe they do know who I am but have no reason to follow up on it. Remember that Charles Bronson movie, *Death Wish*? They figured out who *he* was but because he was knocking off the bad guys; they never went after him."

"Wait... so you're telling me that as long as unsolved crimes are getting solved, they have no interest in how or why?" Lisa fell back on the couch shaking her head.

Right now, all they have is a burner phone number that doesn't have a name attached to it. Whenever I made a call, I was careful to drive out to the edge of town, so that even if they tracked the call, it would lead to a parking lot." Ryan seemed to be unraveling a bit.

"What if one day a SWAT team surrounds my car or barges into our home, or my office? Do you really think anyone's going to believe my story?" He took a deep breath to calm himself before continuing to speak. "Look, I'm always going to have dreams and there's always going to be bad things that happen in the world. Maybe the best thing to do is to just stop acting on it... and we can get back to the way things were."

Lisa didn't know what to say.

"I know," Ryan blurted, "why don't we take a drive on Saturday? Maybe go hiking with the kids? We could all use a change of scenery." Without waiting for a response, he reached for the remote and turned on the TV.

Lisa knew when to speak up, when to debate, and when to just say nothing at all. She also knew that getting away for the day was good idea and probably a great way for the family to reconnect. But she wasn't convinced that anything would change once they returned home.

# Chapter 21

The Field family enjoyed their two-hour hike through Umstead State Park, followed by dinner at the kids' favorite place, Chili's. Meanwhile, the Fulton PD was experiencing a typical weekend night. There was a call reporting a domestic dispute, then a call reporting a fender bender near the high school, followed thirty minutes later by a report of teenagers getting rowdy at the local skating rink. Up until 9:45, it was a fairly quiet night. Then all hell broke loose.

*"Officer down! Officer down! Ray's liquor store, 17th Street and McCray!"* Officer Baines was breathing hard, and his voice was panicked. The call shouted over the police radio echoed throughout the department. A call went out for all units in the area to proceed immediately to Ray's Liquor Store, prompting three Fulton cruisers and the local sheriff to respond. No one could ever recall an "Officer Down" situation in Fulton before.

Officers Baines and Lenox had responded to a robbery in progress at the liquor store, arriving on the scene just as the three suspects bolted from the store and ran toward a darkened alley between the liquor store and a vacant lot. As the two officers flew out of their cars to give chase, the suspects split up, one sprinting through a back parking lot and jumping a fence while the other two ran down the street that ran behind the stores. The two then turned and sprinted through yards.

Seeing the suspects split up, the officers did as well. Baines, being a bit bulkier and not as fast as Lenox, broke off and sprinted in the direction of the lone suspect. He caught a glimpse of the wiry frame thirty or forty yards ahead of him, the distance increasing between them each second. Baines was clearly no match in this foot race and slowed down as the figure disappeared into the night. Lenox, meanwhile, was a marathoner and even though the chase was happening over fences and through backyards, he was swiftly gaining on them.

Still panting from his aborted chase, Baines radioed for his partner. "Lenox, come in. Where are you?" Silence. "Lenox!"

He then ran back to where the two had split off in their pursuit, calling in for backup in the process. Baines didn't feel good about the radio silence. He unstrapped his flashlight and began meandering between houses until he emerged one block over. The road was lit by a lone streetlamp, but there was enough light for him to see several figures standing around parked cars halfway down the block. He sprinted toward them, the light from his flashlight settling on the group as he got closer. They were all looking down at the crumpled body of Officer Lenox lying on the pavement between two parked cars. He was alive but bleeding from the head. The sounds of sirens grew louder as Officer Baines knelt over his partner. "Hang in there buddy, help's on the way."

# Chapter 22

Ryan woke Sunday morning from a deep and uneventful sleep. Lisa nestled closer and rested her head on his shoulder. Neither spoke. His gaze was at nothing in particular.

"You sleep ok?" she asked, hesitant of what she might hear.

"Actually, I did! It's starting to feel good again to wake up in the morning." There was an upbeat tone to his reply.

Lisa stretched and swung her legs over the bed. "You stay put. I'm going to pick us up some croissants and a paper." A quick kiss and she leaped out of bed. She was years past feeling the need to doll herself up before leaving the home; just pull the hair back, throw on a sweatshirt and jeans, and that was it.

A crystal blue sky and crisp morning air of early spring greeted Lisa when she walked outside to her car for the five-minute drive to town. Her first stop was Fulton's premiere bakery, The Bake Shop. She pulled her Chevy Tahoe into an empty space two stores down from the bakery, got out, and was immediately engulfed by the smell of freshly baked bread, luring her and others to the bakery's doorstep. A half dozen croissants, a dozen doughnuts, and a freshly baked rye bread later, Lisa was finally on her way.

She walked around to the passenger side of her Tahoe and placed the baked goods on the front seat. Just one more stop – the Rite-Aid to pick up the Sunday paper. As she lifted one of the Sunday papers from the large stack by the door and walked to the cashier, she overheard a hushed conversation between two well-dressed elderly women near the doorway.

"Horrible! I don't ever recall this happening before," one of them whispered.

"Keep him in your prayers," the other replied.

Lisa noticed the serious expression on their faces but did not hear who they were referring to. She paid the cashier and hurried home.

News tends to spread rapidly in Fulton, and this was no exception. When Lisa arrived home, she dropped the bakery goods on the table and hurried to the family room to see if any major story was being reported in the local news channel's morning news. Moments after turning to the news channel, Lisa heard the words "top story" followed by "local officer in critical condition after responding to a late-night robbery."

She sat on the edge of the couch leaning forward, hands clasped in front of her. "Did you hear about this?" she shouted, not realizing Ryan was just a few feet away entering the family room.

"Yeah...it's been on every local channel for the past fifteen minutes," he said standing close beside her.

In a soft, sad voice she said, "Ryan–"

"I know what you're going to say. I've already been thinking about it. It might be difficult because they were on foot when they got away. There are cameras at the liquor store that should already have a general description...but I'll try."

# Chapter 23

They sat close together listening carefully as the newscaster described what happened. "Officer Christian Lenox is in critical condition and being treated for a severe head injury in a hospital in downtown Raleigh. Investigators continue to pour over video surveillance tapes recorded by all cameras in the area, as well as conducting door to door interviews throughout the neighborhood. The only information gained is from the liquor store owner and Officer Baines, who arrived on the scene with Lenox."

Ryan paced around the house clutching his mug, lost in his thoughts. It was more than just what's happened to the Fulton officer. Ryan couldn't escape the obvious – he had the capability to learn more about what happened. He had been avoiding such thoughts, simply because the gravity of its potential frightened him. Walking into the kitchen, he grabbed a croissant from the bag on the counter and turned toward the door.

"Lisa, I'll be back soon," he said, snatching the car keys and heading out.

Ryan cracked the car windows and purposely left the radio off for the duration of the drive. Ray's liquor store was on the other side of town, not an area he was familiar with, so he relied on the GPS to guide him through the turns and distances to help navigate the drive over. The closer he got, the slower he drove, so that he might create a mental picture of the street, the homes, and any landmarks that stood out. The parking lot to Ray's liquor store was in sight just up ahead. Instead of pulling directly into the lot, he turned onto the driveway leading down the alley next to the store, where it ended at the street running behind it.

Ryan looked both ways before turning onto the worn pavement of a street the city seemed to have forgotten all about. He drove slowly past the old homes and ragged yards that reflected a struggling community whose homes were separated by rusted chain link fencing or wooden fences in disrepair. Residents sitting on creaky front porches, as well as those slowly walking along the side of the road, laid a heavy gaze his way as he drove by, as if to say, *"and what exactly is it you want around here?"* Ryan felt uncomfortable and decided that he had seen enough.

Ryan couldn't get out of there quick enough, but he had seen what he needed to see. The ride back home was quick as he replayed the scene of the liquor store and street in his head as he drove. His mind was razor sharp, and he walked through his mental checklist of what he needed to do. When he arrived home, he saw Jason and a couple of his friends playing basketball in the driveway. Rather than interrupt that, he simply parked in the street.

"Hey Dad, up for a game? We've only got three."

"Sorry, bud, how 'bout a rain check? I've really got some important stuff to take care of," Ryan replied before disappearing into the house.

A quick stop at the fridge for a bottle of water, then directly to his office, shutting the door behind him. He had just familiarized himself with the location and surrounding area, but what he needed was the approximate time that the robbery took place. It would help also if he knew roughly where Officer Lenox was assaulted. An online search provided the rest of what he sought.

# Chapter 24

Lisa and Ryan went about their day without saying much about what happened to officer Lenox. She suspected that he had driven to the neighborhood where the robbery took place but hesitated to ask. She became convinced of it only after he returned home and went directly to his office and closed the door. He apparently didn't notice her sitting in the family room. She had seen this before.

As the day wore on, they both acted as if it was like any other Sunday—a few outdoor projects around the house, dinner, and some family time in front of the tube.

"Is dad ok?" Jason asked his mother, as he grabbed a bag of popcorn from the pantry.

"Yeah, he's fine. Just a lot on his mind about work." This was a safe answer she could always get away with.

Ryan said very little at dinner, skipped dessert, and parked himself in the family room recliner.

*Ray's liquor store...Officer Lenox.*

"Boys, how 'bout we pass on TV tonight and you guys go on upstairs?"

Although Lisa phrased it as a question, the boys got the message loud and clear, said goodnight, and went on their way. Mom didn't often give instructions, but when she did, everyone knew better than to put up any resistance. Lisa could see that Ryan needed some alone time. She finished clearing the kitchen and headed directly to her room to take a shower.

Later that evening while Lisa was in bed reading, Ryan quietly entered and shuffled slowly toward the bed. "Hey hon, sorry I was such a dud tonight. Been thinking about, well...you know."

"Don't be so hard on yourself." She gave him a kiss and turned off her light.

Thirty minutes after they said their goodnights, Ryan was still nervously trying to shut down his brain and allow himself to sleep. *Ray's liquor store...* Eventually, he drifted off. His sleep normally consisted of a myriad of dreams, some bizarre that made no sense at all, while others appeared very real and in vivid detail.

*Ryan was in front of Ray's liquor store standing on the curb roughly ten feet from the entrance. It was fifteen minutes until closing time, and there was only one car in the parking lot. He took note of the car's details and license plate, however, no sooner had he committed these to memory when an elderly gentleman exited the store cradling a bag in his hands. Ryan watched him get into the car and slowly drive out of the parking lot and into the night.*

*Several more minutes passed, before a set of slow-moving headlights approached. The vehicle slowly turned into the store parking lot and, instead of parking, continued suspiciously toward the side of the building toward the alley adjacent to the building, where it came to a stop. Ryan walked toward the vehicle and observed occupants in the front and back. They drove an older, white Ford Explorer with South Carolina license plates. The light that was supposed to illuminate the license plate was out, and he could only see the numbers 147 and the letter X. He also noticed that the passenger side brake light was out.*

*The doors opened in unison, and three young men donning masks, emerged and ran by him. A fourth occupant then slowly drove off. Ryan knew what was about to happen inside Ray's store, but he was more intent on getting a description of the vehicle and what was going to eventually happen to officer Lenox. Any moment he would be hearing the sirens of the police cruisers racing to the scene.*

*Ryan picked up his pace and walked to the end of the alley, turned, and headed up the street. The wail of the sirens grew louder until he was certain they had arrived at the liquor store. He heard car tires screeching and frantic yelling followed by the sounds of panicked feet running toward him. He watched as the three suspects split up; Officer Baines attempting to chase the lone runner, while Officer*

*Lenox was furiously gaining on the other two as they dodged between houses and over a fence. Ryan ran to join them, although he had no sense of touching the ground. As he reached the next block over, he could see that Officer Lenox had stopped on the dark street and carefully approached a cluster of parked cars.*

*Officer Lenox appeared distracted by a sound, turned his head, and in that split second a figure jumped up swinging something that struck the officer on the side of his head. For a moment, the two suspects hovered over the fallen officer who was clearly not moving. Ryan could see that the weapon was an aluminum baseball bat, which was quickly tossed into bushes between the houses. While Officer Lenox lay bleeding on the ground, the two assailants ran off into the night. He stood there for another few moments and watched as a couple walking their dog and several teenagers on bikes stopped to see what was happening. Officer Baines soon joined them.*

Ryan woke abruptly from the dream. He rolled onto his back and laid there rubbing his eyes, processing what he had just seen.

Lisa pushed open the door and walked in to make sure he was awake. She hadn't slept well that night. "Good morning hon," she said in a soft, tired voice. "Sleep ok?"

Ryan knew exactly what she was asking. The tone of her voice, the look on her face.

"Yeah, it took a little while, but I did sleep well. And yes...I was *there*!"

Lisa covered her mouth with her hand. She knew what *there* meant.

Then Ryan said in a flat voice, "I need to purchase a new burner phone on the way to work today."

# Chapter 25

There was a completely different atmosphere inside the police station house in downtown Fulton on Monday. The usual cheery conversation and needling among officers were replaced with solemn looks and awkward silence. One of their own was in the hospital in critical condition and the usual lighthearted mood around the station was gone. Local reporters did their best to stay informed, which meant frequent calls and interview requests flooding the station house. A spokesman for the department attempted to take all questions, shielding the officers from having to deal with the media and allowing them to pursue their investigation.

"Hold on, I'll transfer you now," an exasperated rookie cop said after answering his third call in the past two minutes. Sarah Bunning picked a bad day to be out sick. The phone on Sgt. Ramos's desk rang. Inhaling deeply, he prepared himself for yet another reporter's request for information.

"This is Sgt. Ramos; how may I help you?" he said in a tired tone.

On the other end, Ryan slowly and methodically provided all the information he had *seen* in his dream. It included a description of the suspects, but more importantly, a detailed description of the vehicle and license plate he saw dropping off the suspects. Ryan didn't identify himself and he didn't allow Sgt. Ramos to interrupt. But just as he was finishing up, Sgt. Ramos barked into the phone. "Please, don't hang up. I know you've called in multiple tips before. I know you're local."

The line went silent for a moment and then Ryan responded, "I'll be in touch." Ryan, was startled, hung up the phone, and sat in his car parked outside Research Triangle Park staring at the burner phone in his hand.

*I know you've called in multiple tips before. I know you're local.*

That could only mean one thing; his anonymous tips may not be so anonymous after all. Ryan immediately called his boss Alan Tockett. "Alan, this is Ryan. There's not much on my schedule for this afternoon, so if it's okay with you, I'd like to take off the rest of the day."

"Sure Ryan, not a problem. See you tomorrow." Alan sat back after hanging up the phone. He'd seen a change in Ryan over the past few months, and this was the first time Ryan had ever taken time off in the middle of the day. It was probably nothing, he thought.

It wasn't necessary for Ryan to call ahead, but he wanted to ensure she'd be home when he got there. "Lisa, just letting you know that I took the rest of the day off and I'm on my way home."

"What happened, is everything OK?" she asked. The last time he left work and came home in the middle of the day, it was for a far different reason that resulted in a wonderfully pleasurable experience. Sensing by his voice, however, she wasn't expecting this visit to have the same results.

"We'll talk when I get there," he said. "I made the call and provided all the information they needed. But I'm not comfortable with how the call ended. Anyway, I'll be home in fifteen minutes."

Lisa wasn't sure what to expect when Ryan's car rolled up the driveway and the door flew open. His walk was brisk as he entered the house and paced around the kitchen, barely making eye contact while pulling out a chair at the table and sitting down.

"All right, so tell me what's wrong," Lisa asked.

"I spoke to your friend, Sgt. Ramos. I gave him all the details and then he said something very strange just as I was about to hang up. He said that he *knew* I called multiple times before and that I'm local."

Lisa remained calm and spoke in a soft, yet reassuring tone. "Ryan, we haven't broken any laws, have we? All you've done is helped them. Look, the boys and I met Sgt. Ramos when we volunteered a couple of years ago. He's genuinely a nice guy who loves this community."

Ryan's brow wrinkled. "OK, so what are you getting at?"

Lisa was deliberate in her reply. "Why don't you meet with him? Tell him about what you're able to do. No more burner phones, no more driving off and calling from out of town. One call to him and let him handle everything."

Ryan shook his head slowly and deeply exhaled. He was so against ever revealing this to anyone. "So, when does it all stop, Lisa?"

Her eyes widened and she looked directly at him. "It stops when *you* want it to stop. You can simply say that you're gradually losing the ability to do what it is you do. And then, it's over. Tell him the dreams don't happen anymore, I don't know!"

Ryan forced a laugh. "That might work with our Sgt. Ramos, but I'm not so sure that will work with you! Can you just give me a little time to digest this?"

"Sure. Tell you what...why don't you just sleep on it?"

Realizing what she just said, they both looked at each other and cracked up laughing. A break in the tension felt good, though it wouldn't last long.

# Chapter 26

Sgt. Joe Ramos had planned to visit Officer Lenox in the hospital until he got that call from Ryan. First, he needed to make a call to an old acquaintance with the South Carolina State Police. He had met Captain Abrams about two years ago while working on a homicide that took place in Columbia. The suspect fled to and was eventually apprehended in Raleigh. Since then, the two have collaborated on other cases that crossed state lines.

Captain Rodney Abrams had worked his way up the ranks from his early days patrolling the streets in his Ford cruiser. He grew up in a rough neighborhood, was an above average defensive lineman in high school, and had set his sights on becoming a police officer. At six foot-six inches and weighing roughly 260 pounds, he was an imposing figure who instantly commanded respect.

"This is Sgt. Joe Ramos from the Fulton Police Department in North Carolina. May I speak with Captain Abrams please?"

"Hold one," was the reply.

"Abrams," was how he answered the phone on the first ring. He didn't find the need to waste words, got to the point, and already had a busy schedule to get to.

"Rodney, this is Joe Ramos from Fulton PD."

The voice on the other end got a little friendlier. "Joe, been a while, what can I do for you?"

Sgt. Ramos proceeded to describe the assault on a fellow officer and said he had received a tip that the suspect's car appears to be from South Carolina. He provided Captain Abrams with all the information Ryan had provided about the vehicle and the suspects.

"How's the officer doing?" was the first thing Abrams asked. It didn't matter to him that this officer was from another precinct or that he was in another state. He was one of their own, and he always took it personal when an officer was assaulted.

"He's in the hospital, banged up, but he'll make it."

Abrams immediately shot back, "I'm getting this information to my team now, I'll keep you posted." That was something else Ramos admired about Rodney Abrams; he always referred to the officers under his command as his *team*. Ramos got off the phone and headed to the hospital to check on a member of *his* team.

That afternoon after having checked in on Officer Lenox and relaying his improving condition to other officers in the precinct, a call came in from South Carolina.

"Joe, Abrams here," said the deep, powerful voice on the other end. "We identified the owner of that vehicle you described. A twenty-one-year-old habitual. We're in the process of bringing him in now for questioning."

Ramos was fist pumping the air around him. "That's great. Can you fax me a picture so I can ask my officer to make a positive ID?"

"Not a problem. I'll shoot it up your way shortly."

Ramos hung up the phone, took a deep breath, and leaned back in his chair. He reflected on the anonymous tips he'd received over the past few months. They've been accurate. *All* of them! He didn't see any particular pattern as to when they were received, particular crimes, or specific locations. What really struck Sgt. Ramos, though, was that the caller never sought any credit or financial reward.

A moment later, Sarah Bunning walked by his open office door carrying a handful of folders. "Joe, you've got a call on Line 1," giving him a look as if to say she had no clue who it was.

She left and continued down the hallway, as Ramos glanced at the blinking light on his phone pad. "This is Sgt. Ramos; may I help you?"

"It's your local tipster. It's time we meet."

# Chapter 27

The call was short and to the point, much like all the anonymous tips in the past. There was no small talk, no exchange of pleasantries. The caller asked that Sgt. Ramos meet him that night at a Starbucks in downtown Raleigh at 7 p.m. He preferred Ramos to be out of uniform and to come alone.

This normally would have been a red flag, but Sgt. Ramos didn't seem overly concerned. The fact that he insisted on a very public place to meet was reassuring.

Joe Ramos lived just south of Raleigh and estimated the drive would take roughly twenty minutes to get downtown, then several minutes to park and walk to the Starbucks chosen for this meeting. Experience had taught him to always scout an area prior to any meeting. This would be no different. He heated a pot pie in the microwave at 5:30, threw on a pair of khakis and a bright red polo shirt, and was out the door by six.

Ramos mentally reviewed every phone encounter he had had with the caller. He thought about the tips provided, the types of crimes involved, and how the caller might be linked to it all. Ramos had studied the calls to develop a profile of the caller – Caucasian, 30-40 years old, somewhat educated. The caller appeared to be rational and well-intentioned. Nonetheless, Sgt. Joe Ramos would have his guard up. It just didn't add up.

At 6:15, he found a parking spot two short blocks from the Starbucks on Fayetteville Street. The early evening air was calm, yet sticky, and the sidewalks were filled with pedestrians shuffling between the numerous bars and restaurants lining the street. Ramos blended into the crowd, eyeing everyone around as he approached his destination. The moment he entered, he was hit by the aroma of coffee and the quiet singing of Carole King playing overhead. Straight to the counter, he ordered a latte while surveying all the occupants inside. No one looked at him suspiciously, and it appeared to be the usual coffee shop crowd, he thought to himself.

Ramos found a booth near the window far away from the door, a perfect place to observe anyone entering the establishment. His iPhone showed 6:25 p.m. He sipped his latte and fiddled with his iPhone, as he assessed each person who walked in. A young man, perhaps in his early twenties entered, ordered an iced coffee, and sat in a nearby booth with his laptop. Ramos watched him, tried to make eye contact, but the young man was too engrossed in his laptop. Probably not him. It was almost 7 o'clock.

The front door opens and in walked an attractive brunette with her hair pulled back, wearing an NC State sweatshirt. He thought she looked vaguely familiar but didn't want to stare, so he redirected his gaze out the window. The woman briefly scanned the shop, and once she noticed Ramos in the booth, she walked over and sat down across from him.

"Sgt. Ramos, do you remember me? My sons and I worked a fundraising event with you a few years back, and I got sick and had to leave. You were gracious enough to drop my boys off at home after the event."

He barely had any recollection of what she was describing, and besides, he couldn't be distracted now, he was waiting for his contact to arrive any moment. "You know, I do think I remember that," he said, feigning the truth as he kept an eye on the front entrance. "How are your boys doing?"

"Oh, they're fine," she said, "but that's not why I'm here. I'm here to discuss the tips you've been receiving."

# Chapter 28

This was clearly not the person he'd been talking to on the phone, but there was no doubt she's part of what's going on. "Look, I appreciate any tip I receive, especially when it leads to solving a crime," he began, "but I've got more questions than answers right now."

Ramos wondered why it was *her* that he was talking to, and not the caller who specifically said, *it's time we meet*. He perceived Lisa as truthful and sincere who gave no indication that she wanted anything from him. Still, Ramos thought, *they called this meeting, there must be something more to this*.

"Why exactly did you want to meet, and because it wasn't you that made those anonymous calls, why isn't the person who did make those calls here?"

"I need a coffee. Get you anything?" she asked.

Ramos declined and carefully watched her walk to the counter and place her order. Perhaps getting up and walking to the counter was a signal to someone else sitting nearby or watching from outside? His eyes shifted in all directions. He bit his lower lip and rubbed his brow as he tried to piece together this puzzle based on the bits of information Lisa was supplying. The cop in him decided it was time for some direct questioning. After all, *they* called this meeting. *They* must have something they want to say, admit to, or demand. It was time to be direct.

Lisa returned to the table; her hand wrapped around the dark green cup. His eyes tracked her until she was seated back down.

"Ma'am–"

"It's Lisa. Lisa Field."

"OK, Lisa – can I assume that the caller is your husband?"

Lisa nodded.

"I'm guessing there's a reason why he didn't want to be here, even though he has no reservation about calling me to provide information...information, by the way, that happens to be very accurate and unavailable from anywhere else. Certainly, you can understand my...curiosity."

Lisa took a long sip of her coffee then inhaled deeply. Ramos recognized this body language in people he had interviewed over the years. It told him that she was anxious and on the verge of wanting to convey something of importance.

Lisa fidgeted with her wedding band, and her eyes wandered toward the ceiling, as if searching for words. Ryan had told her that if she felt totally comfortable and could trust Sgt. Ramos, then to just go ahead and divulge everything. What's the worst that could happen, he'd laugh and write her off as a loon?

"I'm not sure where to begin, so I'll just start at the very beginning. Do you remember the very first tip you received?" Before he could answer, she said, "A kidnapped child?"

Ramos instantly nodded, recalling everything about that case.

"I was reading about the kidnapping in my kitchen the morning after it happened. When my husband came into the kitchen, I read him the article. He didn't tell me at the time, but later he told me that he had just awoken from a dream where a little girl was kidnapped."

Ramos sat in silence, his chin in his hand, wondering to himself, *where exactly is this going?*

Lisa sat up a little straighter, made more direct eye contact, and continued. "A day or two later, he found the newspaper article and noted the address of where the abduction took place. He drove over to that neighborhood, located the house, and was shocked to see that *everything* looked exactly as it did in his dream. Exactly! Mind you, he had never been in that part of town before." She paused and took a sip of coffee.

Ramos never took his eyes off her, as she spoke. *The details. How did he get all those details, he thought? He had a dream and drove by a house.*

"OK, this is where it gets a little crazy," she said. "He didn't tell me at the time, but in that dream, he said he was literally standing right there near the driveway when it all took place."

Ramos blinked a few times trying hard not to disregard what he was hearing.

Lisa's voice was now slightly more forceful. "He witnessed *everything* – the child, the mom, the white van, the kidnapper. He even noted the license plate number. When he woke up, he still remembered these details but thought it was just a random dream ...until I read that article to him when he entered the kitchen."

His brow furrowed and mouth slightly open, Joe Ramos was derailed by what he was hearing. He took a moment to think about it. Over the months he had been given anonymous tips that helped to solve multiple crimes, the kidnapping case being the most prominent one. So, this was not a one-time thing.

"Remember now, I'm still in the dark about all of this," she said as her voice lowered. "After my husband returned from locating the house and what he saw there, he said he wasn't feeling well and went to lie down."

Ramos's expression hadn't changed and he looked at her, as if waiting for a punch line.

"Well, forty-five minutes later he comes out of the room after his nap and asks me to read him that article about the missing girl. After I read it, he looks at me almost in shock and says that he was just there *again* – in a dream he just had during that short nap!" By then her voice was almost a whisper, afraid that someone might overhear what she's saying.

"Let me see if I understand what you're telling me," Ramos said. "You're saying that this dream just randomly popped into his head during a nap a day or two after the original dream?"

"No, not *randomly*," she said. "He was consciously thinking about the details of the crime, fell asleep and..." She knew this was sounding bizarre but said it anyway. "He fell asleep and was able to witness the kidnapping again!"

Ramos had both hands clasped in front of him, his elbows on the table, and stared directly at her, as if interrogating a prisoner. After a moment, in a voice that implied he was still having a hard time believing what he was hearing, he asked, "And I suppose he was able to do this repeatedly for all the other tips he provided?"

Lisa simply nodded. "Look, I know this sounds crazy. My husband didn't ask for this, and it's certainly something he doesn't want to go public with."

"I wouldn't even know how to begin to explain this to anyone," Ramos said. "Besides, if the media ever got ahold of a story like this, your life would be hell...and that's *if* they believed you! If they didn't believe you, you'd be humiliated and written off as a whack-job. Anything else I should know?"

Lisa just shook her head.

"OK, let's just stay in touch.

# Chapter 29

Sgt. Joe Ramos sat behind his desk poring through his thoughts from the conversation at Starbucks. Lisa had come across as rational, sincere, and believable. He had watched and listened to her very carefully, taking note of her eye movements, body language, gestures, and every other communications cue he was skilled at observing during interrogations. Nothing jumped out as being misleading.

A light tap on the door interrupted his thoughts. Officer Baines poked his head in. “Hey Sarge, I’m heading over to the hospital on my lunch break to see Lenox. Do you want to ride over together?”

Ramos made it a point to visit his injured officer every day, but his focus was squarely on the previous night’s discussion. “I’m sorry Baines, I’m behind on a few things and need to work through lunch today. Tell Lenox to stop lying around and get back to work.”

Baines chuckled and pulled the door shut as he left. The office was eerily quiet, and the late morning sun lit up the room. He shifted his thoughts back to Lisa Field and the husband he had yet to meet.

Ramos’s thoughts were rapid fire. The story she told was frankly unbelievable. So why then would she want to meet and tell such a tale? Was her husband somehow involved in the crimes or a witness to them, and was she trying to throw him off? Was she testing him for a reaction to see if he would believe it or start asking specific questions to catch her in a lie?

The more Ramos scribbled on his notepad, the less it made sense. He had always prided himself in his ability to solve puzzles, find contradictions, and identify elements that just didn’t belong. He tapped the pencil repeatedly against the desk and shook his head. Nothing. All he had was a crazy story; one he’d never heard before.

This stuff held a hint of science fiction. He needed proof and thought there might be a way to get it. He reached back into a file cabinet behind him where dozens of unsolved cold cases are contained in manilla folders that dated back twenty years. If what Lisa Field had told him was true, then perhaps he could help with one of these? Hell, he could solve them all if what she said was true, he thought facetiously. The folders contained cases of high-profile robberies, home break-ins, assaults, car jackings; it was a smorgasbord of unsolved crimes.

Ramos wrote down a few notes, not about the crimes, but about Lisa Field and what he could infer about her husband. He remembered her mentioning that they had two sons. He then scanned the pages listing the department's unsolved crimes over the years. Turning each page, running his finger slowly down each one, he'd place a red check mark next to any that might be a candidate to use. As he neared the bottom of the fifth page, he didn't draw a check mark; he drew a large red circle.

He pulled out Lisa Field's cell phone number.

# Chapter 30

Lisa's phone rang just before noon, and she didn't know what to think when Joe Ramos identified himself. "Mrs. Field, Sgt. Joe Ramos here" he began.

"Please, call me Lisa," she politely reminded him.

"OK, Lisa - I'm still wrapping my head around everything you told me last night. And I know that your husband has provided information that has helped me solve several crimes; crimes that frankly, we weren't making much progress on."

There was a pause, and Lisa had a feeling she knew where this was going.

"Lisa, we've got dozens of unsolved crimes dating back a couple of decades. And no, I'm not asking your husband to solve all of them. But - if I was to give your husband one of these cases, and he is able to provide new information, it would go a long way in convincing me of everything you told me."

"Let me talk to him tonight," she said.

Ryan had a good day. His manager, Alan Tockett, praised a few of his recommendations for design changes for the rail project's train control system, and a positive annual review at the end of the day promised a nice bump in salary. The drive home was met with traffic congestion in the usual places, but with the radio blaring out hits from the 1980s, even the slow pace of traffic was more tolerable. He hadn't once thought about Lisa's meeting with Sgt. Ramos.

The first thing Ryan noticed when he entered the house through the side door was a bottle of Merlot, two wine glasses, and a cork-screw on the kitchen counter. That usually meant one of four things: she'd had a bad day; the boys had an issue at school; she wanted to make a major purchase for the home; or there was something serious to talk about.

Lisa entered the kitchen right after she heard Ryan enter. "So, how was your day? Wasn't today your yearly review?" Her tone was upbeat.

"Actually, I had a really good day and, yup, had a great review! So, what are we celebrating?" He readied himself for a response.

"I heard from Sgt. Ramos today," she said, uncorking the bottle. "He wants to meet with you and give you a file to look at."

The good day Ryan had been having just took a turn. "Seriously? So now I'm his personal crime solver?" There was bitterness in his voice, and he instantly regretted the decision to contact Joe Ramos, but the damage was done.

"Hon, it's not like that at all. He listened to every word I said, and not once did he fall off his chair laughing." Lisa always had a way of being silly at the right time to lighten the mood.

Ryan stared at her. He shot back, "Did people stare much when he put the straitjacket on you?" They both breathed a little easier now that the tension was eased.

"I mean, if you were him, would you believe this?" Lisa had a point. She always did. She pointed to a piece of paper on the counter. "Here's his cell phone number. Honey, listen, I trust him. He's been in this community for years and even helped us out a few years ago when he drove the kids home from that festival. And besides, *we're* the ones who reached out to him, remember?"

Ryan took the piece of paper and slowly rolled his eyes over the number. He wasn't in the mood to answer a ton of questions. "Okay, okay. No wine just yet, not before I talk to him." He walked down the hall and paced around his office before reaching for the home phone and placing the call. A friendly sounding voice answered on the third ring. "Mr. Field?"

Ryan's jaw dropped. "Uh, yes, this is Ryan Field, how–"

Joe Ramos interrupted. "Sorry Mr. Field, caller ID. It's the world we live in today. Anyway, I'm glad you called."

So much for remaining anonymous, Ryan thought. "So, Lisa told you everything, and you want me to look at a file?" Ryan tried not to sound irritated.

"If you don't mind," Sgt. Ramos replied.

Ryan wanted the meeting to be somewhere quiet where they could talk. "Can you meet me at the library on Hillsborough Street tonight at 6 p.m.?"

"I can. How will I recognize you?"

"Wait by the information desk. Lisa will be with me."

# Chapter 31

The DH Hill Library was huge with an abundance of private rooms and quiet nooks and crannies everywhere. Sgt. Ramos, who had gotten there his usual 30 minutes early, was standing near the information desk at six o'clock, as requested. Ryan and Lisa arrived at 5:55, found a parking spot close to the main entrance, and headed in a few minutes after 6.

Lisa spotted him right away. "The blue pullover sweater standing next to the book cart," she whispered to Ryan, as they eyed the information desk straight ahead. Joe Ramos had already spotted the pair the moment they walked through the double doors. He immediately recognized Lisa and turned his attention to sizing up Ryan. He appeared neither intimidating nor confident, almost as if Lisa was calling all the shots. Their walk quickened as they got closer.

Ryan extended his hand. "Sgt. Ramos? Ryan Field."

Ramos was impressed by the firmness of his handshake. "Mr. Field, nice to meet you," he said as giving a nod to Lisa. "There are a number of small study rooms along the back by the window. We'll have more privacy there." Ramos turned to lead the way, a black leather portfolio tucked under his arm.

The three quietly walked down a wide, carpeted corridor, entering the first empty room they came upon. In the room was a large round table with five chairs and a whiteboard taking up an entire wall. Ramos was the last to enter, closing the door securely behind him. The room was practically soundproof.

"Reminds me of my days back in school," Ryan blurted out to break the silence.

"And where was that?" Ramos asked, feigning interest.

"Down the block at State. But I don't think that's the sort of thing you want to talk about, is it?"

Lisa gave Ryan a look to remind him of the conversation they had on the drive over – and that was *don't act irritated.*

They took seats at the table, Ryan and Lisa next to each other, and Ramos across facing both of them. Sgt. Ramos placed his portfolio on the table, unzipped it, and removed a manilla folder, which he slid across the table. "Mr. Field, let me first start by saying how much I appreciate the information you've provided in the past."

Unlike Lisa, Ryan did not insist that he be called by his first name.

Ramos continued, "And I'll be honest with you, I've thought through every possibility of how you could have attained the information that you did." Everything from the language used, the manner in which they were seated at the table, and the confinement of the room would have you believe this was a formal police interrogation. Ryan sat stoic while he inwardly fumed.

"Look, I mean no disrespect whatsoever, but what your wife told me was beyond what I consider... logical. But – if you can really do what Lisa told me you could do," Ramos then shifted his eyes at the folder, "I would greatly appreciate if you could take a look at this."

"Is this my test? Ryan asked as he pressed his forefinger to the folder. Lisa gave his arm a little squeeze to remind him *again* to stay calm.

"I wouldn't call it a test, it's more like a plea for help," Ramos said in a soft tone. "Please." Ramos knew exactly when to back off and soften his approach.

Ryan opened the folder and began to scan the description of the crime. Lisa and Ramos exchanged a glance, as Ryan continued reading and nervously shifted in the chair. Ramos studied Ryan's face and could see that it was having an emotional effect. The details in the file were gruesome enough to cause Ryan to grimace and shake his head. Finally, he closed the file. "Okay," was all Ryan could say.

Sgt. Ramos had pulled a cold case file that he *knew* would strike a nerve. The case had gone nowhere for just over a year and centered around the abduction and murder of a boy roughly the same age as Ryan's son. The boy had disappeared while walking home after a Little League baseball game. His body had been found two weeks later almost five miles away in an abandoned warehouse.

The three got up and quietly walked out together, parting once they walked through the double doors at the main entrance. Ryan, firmly grasping the folder turned to Sgt. Ramos, "I'll get back to you if..." His voice trailed off.

When they got to their car, Ryan tossed the folder onto the back seat, clearly not wanting to share its contents with Lisa. She had seen the change in his mood once he read what Ramos gave him. His aggression was gone, replaced with a sullen, pensive demeanor. Neither one said a word for almost ten minutes.

"Can you share with me what it is he needs help with?" Lisa finally pleaded.

Ryan had been eager to share everything in the past but was clearly withholding this one back. He recalled that when she was around twelve years old, a classmate of hers had been kidnapped and she was never found. Lisa was so devastated by this that even to this day she's frightful that something like that could happen to one of her sons. And this is exactly the type of case he wants me to look at, Ryan thought as he drove home.

"Can we talk about it when we get home?" was all he could say. And true to his word, when they arrived home, he sat down with Lisa and told her the details of the case that Sgt. Ramos needed assistance with. As he expected, Lisa took it hard. Now, she was the one doubting the decision to involve Sgt. Ramos.

# Chapter 32

The discussion was emotional. The events of the crime described in the folder given to Ryan were an ugly reminder of what happened decades earlier to Lisa's classmate, but what haunted them both even more, was that the missing boy was the same age as their son Aaron. Although neither verbalized it, both believed that Sgt. Ramos seemed to be selective in the case he asked Ryan to help with.

Lisa was first out of bed the following morning after a restless night of sleep. Baking always relieved tension or provided a lift when she was down, so the morning was perfect for muffins. Within thirty minutes, the kitchen and most of the downstairs experienced the muffin's fragrance. The shower in the master bath could be heard and she wondered whether *it* happened last night. Moments later, the trampling of feet down the stairs signaled the imminent arrival of the boys.

"Good morning, guys, how'd you sleep?" Both seemed more eager to attack the plate of warm muffins on the counter than acknowledge their mother. Lisa had already had their lunches made, and packed them into their backpacks. Her goal was to get them on their way as soon as possible so she could speak with Ryan alone. And if Ryan did indeed have *the dream* last night, it might be too emotional for him to speak in front of the boys. Aaron had finished first, ran upstairs to brush his teeth, and was down quickly. Jason decided on a second muffin and was still loitering around the table. Aaron shoved his arms through the loops of his backpack and headed for the door.

"Whoa there!" Lisa barked. "Wait on your brother." She turned to Jason who clearly got the message. He wrapped what was left of his second muffin in a napkin, grabbed his backpack, and joined his brother.

"Bye Mom," they chirped in unison, and bolted out the door.

Several minutes later the sound of slowly approaching footsteps were heard. She looked up with tense eyes as Ryan entered the kitchen with a towel draped over his shoulders, took one look at her and shook his head. There was no need to ask.

"I've got a big day at work today," Ryan said in a tone that implied he wanted no part of the crime discussion. "We're supposed to review the final design for the rail system today, but I received an email late last night saying that the Jim Asom, has called an 'all-hands' meeting at 9 a.m. That's never good news."

Jim Asom was the program manager who seldom had anything positive to say. He always expected everything to go right, so when it did, that was the norm. But if something didn't go according to plan or heaven forbid, a cost or schedule deviation occurred, there would be hell to pay.

Ryan leaned against the granite counter, towel drying his hair and gazing out the window. To Lisa, he looked like he was deep in thought a thousand miles away. He was clearly on edge, and she wasn't sure if it was work-related or a result of that damn folder Ramos gave him to look at.

"Any preference for dinner tonight?" she asked. The request seemed to snap him out of his trance-like thought.

"How about I pick up a pizza from Gino's on my way home," he offered. "Let's just have a casual night tonight, Ok?"

# Chapter 33

Ryan's Camry came to a sudden stop in the driveway and he emerged carrying a large pizza box. The look on his face wasn't one of those "glad to be home" looks.

"This is bullshit," Ryan said when he walked through the door carrying the pizza.

Lately, Lisa had stopped trying to figure out his moods. Sometimes Ryan would want to sit down and talk, other times he'd clam up and retreat to his man cave. Regardless, she tried to find a way to lighten the mood or get him to open up. "Don't tell me they forgot to put the pepperoni on the pizza!" she said playfully feigning anger and hoping to break the tension.

Ryan wasn't always this vocal, but he was clearly pissed off, and this time, Lisa's attempt at humor did little to settle him down. He set the pizza box down on the counter and walked directly to the cupboard and pulled out two wine glasses.

"Join me?" He didn't wait for a response and began pouring two glasses. "Damn city council. Damn politicians. Seems that the rail system we've been busting our asses on for the past eighteen months may not be such a high priority anymore for this area!"

Ryan sighed deeply and sank into the kitchen chair. Without turning to look at Lisa, he continued his mini tirade. "Asom is still fighting for the program but acknowledged that we're in a real dogfight for funding, from both the state and federal sides. The usual budget-cutting bullshit."

Lisa understood she was the sounding board and did her best to diffuse the discussion. "Listen, whatever the outcome is, we'll make it work." And then in a deadpan tone, she added, "If we have to, we can pull the kids out of school, and they can get jobs at Walmart." She waited to see if that would do the trick.

Ryan slowly turned to her with a softer look on his face. "Hmm, what do you think they'd pay an eleven and a fourteen-year-old? Boys, come down here, please." He turned to Lisa. "We could probably get on their medical plan as well!"

Jason and Aaron shoved each other, as they stormed into the kitchen. The smell of Gino's pizza had made its way upstairs and abruptly ended the video war games between them. Lisa placed the pizza box in the middle of the table, scattered plates for everyone, and the four sat down to their favorite pizza, some table chatter about school, homework assignments, and anything else that worked its way in.

***

On the other side of town, Sgt. Joe Ramos was in his kitchen, ready to tackle a plate of reheated spaghetti fresh out of the microwave. A can of Coke and his notebook flanked either side of the plate. He hadn't heard back from Ryan Field and wondered if the "test" he had given him was something Ryan couldn't handle. He began flipping through the pages of his notebook, recounting the tips Ryan provided in the past and how they lined up with the specific details of the crimes. He was unable to find a common link or how it was even possible for Ryan Field to have been physically present when these crimes were committed. Joe Ramos sat there, doing everything he could to look at this logically and *not* believe what Lisa told him about Ryan's dream journeys.

Ramos dragged a slice of bread across his plate to clean the remaining sauce, then took a long gulp of Coke. He turned to the last entry in his notebook which described the meeting he had at the library: *wait three days – if no response about the case, request polygraph*. He would take the chance of insulting Ryan Field with this request, but surely, he'd understand the reason for it. Tomorrow is day two.

# Chapter 34

The glass and steel structure with dark green trim hid behind rows of tall pine trees and a well-manicured landscape inside the 440 Beltline on the southwest side of Raleigh. This branch of the Federal Bureau of Investigation had become one of the most sought after by agents looking to relocate to the southeast part of the country.

Agent Mike McShea, 38 years old and single, had grown tired of his assignment at FBI headquarters on Pennsylvania Avenue in the nation's capitol. Both his father and mother had worked in Washington; his father was an analyst for the FBI, and his mother wrote software programs for government databases. Mike's older brother, Kevin, was a decorated cop in Maryland. In high school, Mike was more passionate about his beach tan and lived in his brother's shadow when it came to academics, sports and girls. So, when his brother graduated and opted to become a cop, Mike saw a career in the FBI as doing him one better.

For eight years, Mike gave the appearance of being a highly successful, hardworking, gritty agent, always trying to make a name for himself. He preferred to work alone, eat lunch by himself, and seldom interacted with colleagues outside of work. Regardless of his personal habits, he always seemed, somehow, to get all the breaks in cases and have the answers when asked. Because of this, he earned the respect of his superiors. That's why they were shocked when Mike put in for a transfer to Raleigh, providing no specific reason other than wanting a change in scenery, and perhaps the last stop before his eventual retirement.

# Chapter 35

Lisa opened her eyes but refused to push herself to get out of bed right away. The large digital numbers on the clock radio showed 6:25, five minutes before the alarm was set to go off. She was normally an early riser, out of bed long before Ryan woke up, but not today.

Sunlight streamed through the kitchen blinds and reflected off the white kitchen cabinets, tearing into Lisa's puffy red eyes as she dragged her feet into the kitchen. Coffee. The boys, all three of them, should be waking up soon, and Lisa needed a quiet moment to herself to power down some caffeine before the kitchen became filled with clanging dishes, and random chatter. But it was too late.

"Good morning, Mom," Aaron said with a quiet smile, as he walked to the pantry to retrieve a box of Cocoa Puffs.

She looked over at Aaron admiring his morning ritual. Why is he always in such a cheery mood in the morning, she wondered. "Good morning," she said with forced enthusiasm.

"Mom, can I–" Aaron said before he was cut off by Jason entering the kitchen.

"Mom, Grant, Robbie, and I need to get to school a half hour early on Wednesdays and Fridays for our science club. Aaron said he's not going to leave a half hour early with us."

"Can't I just walk by myself to school like everyone else does?" Aaron pleaded. "What am I gonna do for half an hour before I have to be in homeroom?"

Lisa was thrilled that Jason had friends down the block and that they all chose to walk to school together every morning. There was safety in numbers, a lesson Lisa learned a long time ago. She wasn't in the mood for this discussion, though. "Aaron, I'm sure your homeroom is open, and for those two days a week can't you read, do some homework, anything for thirty minutes?"

Aaron didn't bother to respond in the losing argument.

Neither boy said another word, finished their breakfast, and scurried back upstairs to get ready for school. Lisa sipped her coffee and wasn't aware Ryan had entered the kitchen until she heard him grab a cup out of the cabinet.

"Good morning sleepyhead," Lisa said  but stopped there, noticing how pale he looked.

He said nothing, just shuffled slowly to the table clutching an empty cup.

"Ryan?" Lisa asked in a soft voice. He turned his head and appeared to be searching for words.

Sitting down, he looked up at her. "That boy – Kevin Conlin – oh God!" was all he could say. He was referring to the boy in the file that Ramos had given him.

"Kevin Conlin?" Lisa was puzzled for a brief second before realizing Ryan had had *the dream*. He looked dazed and struggled to catch his breath before he resumed speaking.

"Lisa, do you think we're ever meant to know everything that happens in life?" he said in a low, distant tone. He then rested his head in his hand and looked straight ahead at nothing in particular.

What do you mean?" she asked, even though she was quite aware of what he was asking.

"I was there; I was right there watching! Remember the file that Ramos gave me about the boy? The last time he was seen was after a baseball game. A teammate saw him walking home...Well, that's where I was. The game had ended, and as everyone started to go their separate way, I focused my eyes on Kevin Conlin. He was among the last to leave. He carried his glove in one hand, his bat on his shoulder, and walked across the street." Ryan stopped talking and turned his eyes upward as if to recall the mental picture in his head. "I followed him. Then, a vehicle slowly approached us from behind and pulled up alongside the boy. The window rolls down and after a few brief words, the boy, without any hesitation walks around to the passenger door, opens it, and gets in."

"It sounds like the boy knew who the driver was."

Ryan looked up at her in disbelief. "Lisa, it was a *police* car!"

"So, isn't that a good thing?" she innocently asked.

"Lisa, that file that Ramos gave me mentioned nothing about any policeman having contact with the boy. And why would he even get in the car if he only lived a few blocks away?"

# Chapter 36

As soon as he arrived at work, Ryan dropped his briefcase off on his desk, put his lunch away, and went directly to the daily 8:30 meeting held in the main conference room. Every day, the project leads would present the current status of the rail project – issues, schedules, and budget. Rumors were circulating that the entire program was on the governor's chopping block and perhaps this would be addressed in the morning meeting. Ryan had a difficult time focusing while he sat near the back of the room pretending to listen. His mind kept going back to *Kevin Conlin*. None of the rumors about the project were addressed. He pulled out his iPhone to check his schedule for the rest of the day. He had to get out of there.

The meeting was over by eleven o'clock, and Ryan marched into Alan Tocket's office directly after to request some personal time off after lunch. "Sure. Is everything ok?" Tocket asked, noticing that Ryan looked tired. He was a solid performer on the contract and seldom asked for time off.

"Yeah, I just need a little time today to take care of a few things at home." His boss noted that this was the second time Ryan has asked for time off, something he hadn't done in the past several years unless it was for a planned vacation. Ryan walked back to his office to check emails and to confirm that he didn't have any deadlines to meet that day. At noon, he packed up his briefcase and called it a day.

"Hey Lis, just a heads up, I'm on my way home," he said as leaving the parking lot. It was unusual for Ryan to leave work in the middle of the day, especially considering the status of the rail project right now. Lisa was sure it had to do with their conversation that morning. That's all *she* thought about since he left.

Twenty minutes later, Ryan walked in looking no more energetic than when he left that morning.

"Get you anything?" Lisa asked, as she met him at the door.

"No thanks. I just want to sit for a while and think about what happened last night. I have to be absolutely certain of what I saw before I go any further with this." Ryan knew that Ramos was having difficulty believing all of this. *What's he going to think now when I implicate a cop?*

He spent the next two hours in his office scribbling down notes, trying to recall every detail. It was almost 3 o'clock when he reached for his cell phone and punched in the number for Joe Ramos.

"Hello?" answered Joe, not mentioning Ryan's name even though it came up on his caller ID.

"Sgt. Ramos, Ryan Field."

"Ryan, please call me Joe. What can I do for you today?" he said in a formal police tone. Joe Ramos held his breath, hoping that the reason for the call was that Ryan had something to say about the file of the missing boy.

"Can we meet... tonight?" Ryan asked. "I'd rather not have this discussion over the phone." Joe Ramos knew better than to push for any details right now. If Ryan had nothing for him, he wouldn't want to meet just to say that. Ramos was excited by the call but kept a calm voice. "Of course, where would be good for you?"

Ryan thought for a moment. "There's a Taco Bell on Highway 64 at the Apex exit. Do you know where that is?"

Ramos was intrigued that he wanted to meet out of town, but he wasn't going to question it.

"Is 7 o'clock ok?" Ryan asked.

"Sure, I'll see you at 7. Tacos on me!"

# Chapter 37

Ryan arrived twenty minutes early and noticed plenty of empty booths. There was a short line at the counter, so he went directly there and ordered a Coke. Patrons were scattered randomly among the tables, but an unoccupied booth in the corner against the window looked to be the best option. Coke in one hand, manilla folder in the other, he slid into the booth and waited for Ramos to arrive.

There were questions that bothered him all day. Why had Joe Ramos given him *this* particular file? He was no dummy, and he could see that Ramos wasn't either. Was it because Ryan had a son around the same age? Ramos was a good cop for a reason. He listened, he empathized, and he appeared to think through all the details, and whether it was a facade or not, he came across as a genuinely nice guy.

*Does Ramos already suspect that a cop was involved?* Perhaps Ramos has an inkling about this already and is testing him to see if he reveals the same suspicion? There was never any mention in the file or public statement that a cop may have been involved. Ryan had another burning question and that was, *where will Ramos's loyalty be if he's told a cop is involved*?

Ryan sat, wringing his hands and beginning to perspire. He was aware that he would have to calm his nerves because Ramos would pick up on that immediately and wonder, *why is he so nervous*?

The sun was getting low in the sky and was now shining directly into the booth. Patrons had arrived, finished their meals, and left, while Ryan just sat there with his drink. Finally, at 7 o'clock sharp, Joe Ramos walked in wearing an NC State baseball cap, looked immediately at the corner booth, gave a nod, and headed over.

Joe Ramos sat down, but before he could say anything, Ryan lobbed the first question his way. "What do *you* think happened to

Kevin Conlin and who do *you* think might have been involved?" Ramos was taken back a bit when Ryan skipped the pleasantries and launched right into the case file. Ryan carefully watched for any reaction to his question. Joe Ramos, however, knew enough about interrogation techniques to know that Ryan knew more than what was in the file and was waiting to hear a response.

"Classic pedophile abduction," Ramos replied in a flat, unrevealing answer. "We scoured the area within 50 miles to identify all known pedophiles, however, one by one we were able to eliminate them as suspects." Maybe Ramos really *doesn't* have a clue about a cop being involved, Ryan thought.

"We checked with neighbors, store owners, friends of the family, anyone who might have had any connection whatsoever to the Conlin family – nothing. My only guess was that it was someone from out of town who then hightailed outta here and disappeared." His voice trailed off, and he shook his head. "And that's sort of where we left it."

Ryan had listened intently and sat in silence. Now, Ramos pointed the question back at him. "Well, you asked to see me. Anything at all?" Ryan inhaled deeply and slowly exhaled, looking around as if everyone had suddenly gone quiet to listen. Ryan immediately noticed one thing different about this meeting and that was that Joe Ramos was taking notes.

"Last night," Ryan began, "I was there. I followed the Conlin boy from the ballfield right after the game. He crossed the street with his glove and bat and started down the sidewalk – nothing out of the ordinary. Until, that is, a car pulled up alongside him and came to a stop." Ryan purposely did not identify the car as a police car. He was still searching Ramos for a reaction. "I wasn't close enough to hear the conversation, but it appeared friendly. After a few moments, the boy simply walked around the front of the car to the passenger door, opened it, and got in."

Ramos had already assumed that this was an abduction, so

hearing about a car didn't really surprise him. "So, that means he may have known the person and voluntarily got into the vehicle? I assume you can identify the car and its plates."

Ryan was quick to respond but not to the question about the car's identity. "I'm not so sure he knew him, but he certainly felt comfortable enough to get into the car."

Ramos shook his head. "That doesn't make sense. His parents assured me that their son was bright enough never to get into a vehicle with someone he didn't know."

"Perhaps, but he obviously felt comfortable enough to get into a *police car*."

That comment completely derailed Joe Ramos's train of thought, and he stopped scribbling on his pad. Ryan then looked him dead in the eyes, "It was a Fulton police car – number 281."

Joe Ramos put his hand over his mouth and slowly shook his head, as if unsure of what he just heard. He then mumbled, "That's why we hit so many dead ends." He wrote something on his pad and looked up at Ryan. "Are you're sure about the car number – 281?"

"Yes, absolutely. Aside from that, I don't have anything else."

# Chapter 38

FBI Agent Mike McShea closed his office door, loosened his tie, and took a seat behind the desk. Directly in front of him, hanging on the wall, was a picture of a 54-foot Bertram cabin cruiser docked in Key West, a seasoned captain with a woman on each arm, and the sun setting in the background. Mike often lost himself daydreaming about being in that picture. *One day it'll happen*, he thought.

Agent McShea had investigative interests in multiple cases which obligated him to work with junior agents in the office. For most of those cases, he provided guidance; in other cases, he delegated the assignments. Of course, if any of those cases happened to get solved, he made sure he was first in line to receive the credit. Typical Mike McShea motus operandi.

A folder was kept on the corner of his desk that contained a unique collection of cases that only agent McShea worked on. These cases consisted of half a dozen nearby crimes, and a few far away that had been solved with the help of anonymous tips. Nothing was unusual about receiving anonymous tips. What was unusual, was that these tips were being called in to a specific police department and to a specific officer, Sgt. Joe Ramos. And they all resulted in crimes being solved.

Why this department? Why this officer? Some of the tips were for crimes far from this officer's jurisdiction. McShea was intrigued by the circumstances enough to compile all the case files for those crimes. The only common thread that ran through all of them was a sergeant in the Fulton Police Department. That seemed like a good place to start.

# Chapter 39

Joe Ramos said goodbye to Ryan, walked out, and sat in his Ford pickup near the Taco Bell entrance. He was never one to jump to conclusions and certainly wouldn't start now. The file clearly stated that the last sighting of the boy was by a teammate as they left the ballfield. If a Fulton cop gave him a ride home, why wasn't that information ever provided? And since when do cops drive around side streets giving kids a ride home? Ramos was driving himself crazy with these questions and needed to get back to the station house to search for answers.

At 8:45 p.m., Ramos's pickup truck cruised into the precinct parking lot. Officers Kurtz and Hildebrandt were heading out the back door of the precinct to their patrol cars for their routine nightly patrol. Ramos exited his truck and made a beeline for the door.

"Hey Sarge, forget something?" Kurtz inquired.

"Yeah, I left a couple of folders on my desk I meant to take home. You guys have a good night," and Ramos marched in through the back door and disappeared. A few heads looked up as Ramos entered and briskly walked directly to his office. It wasn't all that unusual for him to show up at odd times. After all, he was single, had no family in the area, and sometimes he'd just show up at the station when he got bored to hang out with the guys. This time was different though.

He flicked on the light and walked to his desk, where a crumpled wrapper and beverage cup from McDonalds remained from earlier in the day. He powered up his computer and pushed everything else on his desk off to the side. As the screen flickered to life, he punched in the multiple passwords required for Fulton's personnel database. All he had to go on was a patrol car number – 281.

The first piece of information entered was the date that Kevin

Conlin was last seen – June 8, 2017. Ramos then identified all the names of the officers on the Fulton Police Department roster at that time. The department consisted of six patrol cars used for patrolling the streets of Fulton, that for some odd reason, were numbered 280 through 285. Ramos dug deeper and found the shift logs which indicated which officers were on duty and what vehicle they were assigned to. *Vehicle 281 – Officer Bret Timmons*.

He stared at the name for a moment, then recalled that this was the officer who had committed suicide in September 2017, three months after the disappearance of Kevin Conlin.

# Chapter 40

Back in 2014, the Fulton Police Department had received an increase in budget that provided for the addition of two officers to its staff and the purchase of two new vehicles. One of the officers was a recruit right out of the academy and the other was a transfer coming in from Phoenix whose name was Bret Timmons.

Sgt. Joe Ramos made it a point to acquaint himself with every new officer in the precinct, perform his own personal assessment, and provide "guidance" on how they did things in Fulton. Ramos understood how recruits out of the academy wind up in a small town like Fulton as their first assignment; he just wasn't sure why someone from a large city in a very different part of the country would want to transfer here.

Over the next few years, Officer Timmons made every attempt to fit in, but he had a quiet, shy demeanor and usually kept under the radar. He was twenty-eight years old, single, and kept to himself after hours. He showed up to work, did what he was asked to do, and seemed to get along with his fellow officers and the community. Basically, no red flags.

Ramos pulled up the personnel file of Officer Bret Timmons, but there was little there regarding his tenure in Phoenix. He pushed his chair back from the desk to stretch his legs and as he did, a sudden thought came to mind. It had only been a few years, so Ramos was hopeful that someone at the Phoenix precinct might remember Officer Timmons and provide more about his background. He looked up the number and dialed the Phoenix department where Timmons had transferred from.

"This is Sergeant Cahill," answered a friendly voice.

"Sgt. Cahill, this is Sgt. Joe Ramos with the Fulton Police Department in North Carolina. I was hoping you could provide me with some information about an officer who used to work in your precinct?"

"Sure, what's his name?"

"Officer Bret Timmons. I see here in his file that he transferred from your department in 2014."

The response was immediate. "Yes, I remember Officer Timmons. A good cop, he joined us right out of the academy – I think around 2010, give or take a year."

"Can you tell me anything about his personal life and why he asked for a transfer?" Ramos knew he was pushing the boundary by requesting an officer's personal information over the phone, so he anticipated a little pushback.

"May I ask the reason for the inquiry?" Cahill said.

"I'm not sure if you're aware that Officer Timmons committed suicide around a year ago, but there are some questions about whether he might have been involved in something we're investigating." Ramos was purposely vague.

After a brief pause, Cahill replied, "I'm sorry to hear that. He seemed friendly, did his job, and was visible in the community, especially with kids as a coach in Little League baseball."

Ramos' ears perked up at the obvious link to kids and baseball. "Any reason why he might want to transfer to North Carolina? Perhaps he had family nearby?"

"To the best of my knowledge, he didn't have family here in Phoenix. I think he grew up in Minnesota if I'm not mistaken." Cahill paused again before continuing. "There's only one real incident I can recall, and it occurred just a few months before he put in for a transfer. He got into a nasty dispute with a parent of one of the kids he coached. You know, the typical stuff parents like to argue about – how much playing time their child gets, what position he plays, and who knows what else." Ramos knew there was more and pressed the phone firmly against his ear.

"Well," Cahill continued, "I guess it escalated with some words between the two and finally the parent decides to pull his kid off the team. I remember one day Timmons was in the break room telling the story of how some jackass dad in the stands got upset because his kid was always stuck playing the outfield and last in the batting order, so he pulled him off the team. Timmons said he felt like pounding that guy but thought better of it. Turns out the parent was an FBI agent here in town.

"And then I heard something I wasn't meant to hear when I passed by Timmons talking to another officer – 'Manny Montoya, chubby little Mexican kid, just wasn't that good.' I remember when I heard that, I walked over to Timmons and told him to follow me to my office. Let's just say he got a nice little talking to about what is and what isn't appropriate to say."

Ramos listened intently and could see just from that one utterance Timmons made, what it revealed about his character.

Cahill wasn't done yet. "So, a few weeks after our little chat, Timmons puts in his transfer request to the Fulton Police Department. Maybe a week or so after that, I got a call from FBI agent Montoya, the kid's dad. He was looking for Timmons but didn't want to get into any details. I told him that the officer had just transferred to Fulton. And that was the last I heard from either one of them."

Ramos had been furiously taking notes right up until Cahill stopped speaking. "Sgt. Cahill, I appreciate you taking the time to speak with me. You've been very helpful." He hung up and leaned back in his chair exhausted. He shoved the notes into his desk drawer, locked it, and called it a night.

What Sgt. Cahill didn't know was that after he informed FBI Agent Montoya that Timmons had transferred to Fulton, the agent decided to make a call to his FBI counterparts in Raleigh. Whatever had transpired between Timmons and Montoya, the FBI agent wasn't about to let it go.

When Agent Montoya called the Raleigh office, the agent who picked up the phone on the other end was Mike McShea.

# Chapter 41

Jimmy Buffett crooned *Margaritaville* while Joe Ramos cruised the backroads to his apartment. Everything Sgt. Cahill told him fit the profile of the cop that Ryan had described, but that didn't prove Officer Timmins was involved in the disappearance of Kevin Conlin. Ramos pulled into his apartment complex and coasted to a stop in his assigned spot. One more call needed to be made in the morning.

The call desk phone at FBI Headquarters in Phoenix rang just after 8 a.m. "May I speak to Agent Montoya please," Ramos asked, not knowing if the agent was even assigned there anymore.

"Transferring," was the reply. Ramos heard the familiar *click* and *buzz* of his call being transferred.

"Agent Montoya, how may I help you?" The voice was deep and firm.

"Agent Montoya, my name is Sgt. Joe Ramos from the Fulton Police Department, North Carolina. I'll be brief. I'm calling in reference to a police officer who you might have known. His name is Bret Timmons, and he was a cop in Phoenix before transferring to my department several years ago. I believe he was also a Little League baseball coach."

There was an awkward pause. "I remember the officer," was all Agent Montoya said. Then, after another pause, he added, "So, what is it you want to know about him?"

Ramos had his notes in front of him from the discussion he had with Sgt. Cahill about Timmons. Now he wanted to see if what Montoya says lines up with his notes. "Officer Timmons *may* have been involved in a crime here in Fulton. A young boy was involved." Ramos let those words sink in.

"There's something wrong with that son of a bitch–"

"Agent Montoya, Officer Timmons committed suicide just over

a year ago, shortly after the disappearance of a twelve-year-old boy."

Montoya toned down his aggression. "Look, he was my son's baseball coach. We had a little run-in at one of his games, and it appeared to everyone that I was the typical parent in the stands being a jerk. Regardless, I pulled my kid off the team. But I watched him all season how he interacted with the kids. Something wasn't right about him, but I couldn't pinpoint it. There were times I'd follow him after the game. He'd go to parks, the bowling alley, the mall – always alone and always interacting with young boys."

Then Agent Montoya focused in on Ramos. "So, is this some cold case you're trying to solve? And since you said he *may* have been involved, then you really don't have any proof. Are you sure it was suicide? Very well could have been a parent of some kid he was getting too friendly with!"

This caught Ramos off guard. "Uh, that's what's in the report, that's all I know. Anyway, I won't take up any more of your time. I believe that what you've told me fits the narrative. Thanks Agent Montoya, you have a good day."

Ramos stared at the three pages of notes he compiled from his discussions with Ryan, Sgt. Cahill, and Agent Montoya. He was in a bind. One says he *heard* about an altercation at the ballfield and a racial slur in the breakroom. Another strongly *thinks* something is behaviorally wrong with him, and another sees everything in a dream! And unfortunately, the guy in question is dead.

The only reason Ramos got involved in this case to begin with was to "test" Ryan Field's outrageous claim about seeing things in his dreams. He had, after all, provided numerous accurate tips over the past months, so maybe there *was* something to Ryan's claim. Montoya was right about there not being any hard proof, but there *was* something that could be looked into that hadn't been done. He could summon cell tower records of Officer Timmons' calls and cell phone location.

The cop inside of Joe Ramos wanted desperately to pursue this, even if it meant implicating a fellow officer. However, even if Timmons' cell phone showed up at that warehouse where the boy was found, although it might solve the crime, there would be questions as to what led Ramos to look at Timmons to begin with. As much as it pained him, he decided, at least for now to let it go.

# Chapter 42

When agents needed to collaborate with Mike McShea, they always tried to request the meeting to be anywhere except his office. Whenever you were in his office, he made you feel as if you were a child visiting a relative whose house was filled with antiques, new furniture, and spotless walls that you dare not touch or go near. The chairs in McShea's office were purposely arranged two feet in front of his desk and it was essential that they not be moved. The desk was not to be touched, a mistake made by one young agent who dropped a folder onto the desk, which accidently moved McShea's nameplate and knocked over a cup holding his pens.

The standing white board, located at a 45 degree angle from the desk and exactly 16 inches from the wall, contained a perfectly drawn grid of columns and rows detailing the status of several cases that McShea was following. A round wooden table with four chairs appeared undisturbed in the corner. The trash can, which was always empty and clean, sat idly by the door. When seated, Mike McShea could see everything: the door, his white board, the parking lot through the window, and of course, that picture of "his" boat on the wall in front of him.

The phone rang at 2:45 p.m. "Agent McShea, this is Special Agent Del Montoya in our Phoenix office."

"Agent Montoya, what can I do for you?" The name and the office location seemed vaguely familiar.

"Not sure if you remember, but I called you about a couple years ago in reference to a local cop who transferred from Phoenix to your area. His name was Officer Bret Timmons. He was someone I had felt a little uneasy about, and he left here abruptly and landed in your area."

"Oh yes, I remember now." As a professional courtesy, McShea had conducted a cursory check after receiving that call a year ago, but nothing ever came of it.

Montoya continued, "Well, yesterday out of the blue, I received a call from a police sergeant from Fulton, North Carolina, asking questions about this particular officer. He was a bit vague but said Officer Timmons might have been involved in a crime in your area. He was requesting some background information, even though the officer has since committed suicide."

McShea was curious but still wasn't sure why this phone call was directed at him. "So, let me see if I understand this. This officer transferred from Phoenix to Fulton, *may* have been involved in some sort of crime, and is now dead. So, what exactly are you asking me to do? Can you tell me anything about the crime?"

Agent Montoya knew he was speaking with another trained FBI agent who understood what questions to ask and how to ask them. "Ok, I knew this officer personally. He was my son's baseball coach. Just my instincts, and they've always been good instincts - but something wasn't right about this guy when it came to kids."

While Montoya spoke, McShea was busy searching through his personal computer files. He did a search on the word *Phoenix* and *Montoya*, and up popped a file of a phone conversation they had back in 2014. When he opened the file, it contained the officer's name and a brief note about "keeping an eye on him." No other details were provided.

"I don't believe you mentioned that in your first call to me," McShea confidently replied.

"Well, there was no investigation, and the guy was transferring away from here, which I was glad for. But I still felt that this guy should be on your radar. And now I get this call from one of your local cops there saying he may have been involved in a crime involving a child."

McShea saw the relevance of the call. "Can you give me the name of the cop that you spoke with?"

"Ramos. Sergeant Joe Ramos from Fulton Police Department."

# Chapter 43

McShea was familiar with the name *Ramos* – the Fulton cop who personally receives anonymous tips and solves cold cases – and now he's making calls to an FBI office in Phoenix inquiring about a local cop who committed suicide a year ago?

McShea got up and made his way down the hallway in search of a particular rookie agent. He inspected each cubicle nameplate until he found who he was looking for. "Agent Henderson, got a moment?"

"Yes sir, c'mon in," the young agent said in a distinct tone of respect.

Jared Henderson had been an agent for a year but was still regarded as *the rookie*.

After graduating from the FBI Academy, he was only one of four new graduates assigned to the Raleigh field office, and the only African American. Before heading to his new assignment, Jared's dad sat him down and gave him some very sage advice. He told him that as progressive as this nation has become, you still need to work harder than everyone else, always keep your eyes open, and above all, learn everything you can about the people you work with and for.

"How are you enjoying the work in this area?" McShea asked, feigning interest.

"So far, so good," was Henderson's reply, knowing full well Mc-Shea wasn't there on a social visit.

"If you've got some time, I'd like you to perform a background check for me. The subject's name is Sergeant Joe Ramos of the Fulton Police Department. Handle whatever you find as confidential and report back only to me. Feel free to contact me at any time if you have any questions."

"Will do," was all agent Henderson said, as McShea abruptly

turned and walked out. *A background check on a local cop and report back only to him? And keep it confidential?* This certainly peaked the rookie's interest. It was certainly more interesting than the searching through the fingerprint database that he'd been doing for the past week.

Jared Henderson was familiar with all the pertinent FBI databases, in addition to accessing university records, bank records, the IRS, court records, and whatever else he thought of. And if Agent McShea asked him to look into an officer of the law, it must be important. Henderson made this his number one priority.

# Chapter 44

Two weeks had passed since Ryan met with Sgt. Joe Ramos to discuss the Kevin Conlin case. He hadn't heard back from Ramos and wasn't in any hurry to reach out to him. Ryan spent less time locked away in his office chasing stories and more time with Lisa and the boys. Jason and Aaron were glad to have more "dad time," shooting hoops in the driveway, playing board games at night, or just laughing and telling stories around the dinner table. Lisa, however, noticed one thing very different about Ryan – his late-night habit of having an extra drink or two.

Jason filled one large plastic bowl with popcorn and a second with chips. Aaron grabbed two cans of Coke and the two of them disappeared up the stairs to the playroom. Ryan loitered around the kitchen waiting for Lisa to finish her phone call with her mother.

"I assume you're joining me?" he asked her, as she hung up the phone, two wine glasses in his hand.

"Ya know, I think I'll pass tonight. But I'll join you in the family room." Her reply signaled a serious discussion was coming. Ryan settled into the La-Z-Boy, ignoring the nearby TV remote. Lisa walked in, took a seat on the couch, and tucked her legs under her. There was silence, except for the distant shouts and movements coming from the upstairs playroom.

"Ryan, you haven't said much about what's going on – and I don't mean about work. Are you okay?" Lisa's voice was soft but direct.

"Hon, I don't know what to think anymore." He sipped his wine and set the glass down on the end table. "A few days after I talked to Joe Ramos about Kevin Conlin and that cop, I went to bed thinking about nothing except that day when the boy was last seen. And you know what?" Ryan sat up straight. "I was right back there at that ballfield watching it all over again. The following night I had trouble going to sleep because that kid was on my mind. And... I went there *again* that night! The next night before bed, I tried relaxing with a glass or two of wine."

"I didn't know," was all she could say.

"Anyway, after a little wine, I fell asleep faster and without much thought. And what I found was that by having a little wine before bed, I'd fall asleep easier because I wasn't thinking so much. And I wasn't having that dream, or any dream for that matter."

Ryan leaned back in the La-Z-Boy, tilted his head back, and stared at the ceiling. Lisa hated to see her husband like this, yet as much as this all seemed to torment him, it fascinated her. *He can go to bed at night and dream himself to a specific place and time.*

# Chapter 45

Lisa Field had gotten used to watching her husband embrace a glass of wine most nights, and although she was still uncomfortable with it, at least he didn't seem as stressed out about going to bed. After their discussion that night in the family room several weeks earlier, Ryan finally promised to scale it back and deal with whatever dreams he'd have.

Joe Ramos sat at his desk thinking how he hadn't heard from Ryan in almost three weeks. Ramos was still contemplating what to do with the information Ryan gave him about officer Bret Timmons and the Conlin kid. He thought about closing the file and leaving it as a cold case, but for the time being, left the folder in his top desk drawer for easy access. The issue at the forefront of his mind right now was what to do about Ryan Field.

***

Across town in the partially obscured FBI building, Agent Jared Henderson was compiling his notes from two weeks of database searches and countless phone conversations regarding *Joe Ramos*. The deeper he looked, the more interesting it became. McShea was on to something, but Henderson still couldn't understand why the need for confidentiality. Regardless, he would oblige the senior agent's request. It added to the mystique of his research and frankly, was the most exciting thing he'd done in his short time at the Raleigh office.

Jared Henderson reached for his phone. "Agent McShea, this is Jared Henderson, down the hall." McShea sounded busy in his reply. "Uh, yeah Jared, what can I do for you?"

"I've completed the research you requested. Can we meet to discuss?"

McShea's tone instantly changed, "Absolutely. How about ten minutes in my office?" McShea hung up and pulled the Ramos file from his desk drawer, noting the half dozen or so cases where Ramos received tips that led to cases being solved. He also reviewed the notes he took during the conversation he had had with FBI Agent Montoya, who told him about Ramos inquiring about a local cop. McShea was confident that if there was more to this, Jared Hender-son would find it.

Exactly ten minutes later, there was a knock at the door.

"C'mon in," beckoned McShea. In walked Jared Henderson with a thick folder in his right hand as McShea motioned him to sit at the table in the corner. Agent McShea walked around from his desk, ensured that the door was closed tight, and sat at the table across from agent Henderson. "So, what have you got for me?"

"Honestly sir, a lot. I started with the social security number and found that it associates with the name Joe Ramos beginning in 1982. There is no job history for Joe Ramos prior to 1982. I ran a simple check of his fingerprints and initially found nothing. But then I ran them through the AFIS to see what that turned up. Those prints matched a petty thief and suspected drug runner from Juarez, Mexico. The name on that file is Jose Ramos Alvarez."

McShea leaned back in his chair processing what agent Henderson had just said. "You've kept this to yourself?"

"Of course, as you requested," Henderson was quick to reply.

"You've done good work. I'd like to keep that folder if you don't mind. Make sure you safeguard anything on your computer regarding this, understand?" It was less of a request and more of an order.

"Yes sir." Henderson understood the meeting to be over, got up and let himself out.

McShea wasn't quite sure how all this new information tied into all those anonymous tips and the call to Phoenix, but he thought this might be a good time to give "Joe Ramos" a call.

# Chapter 46

Ryan had kept his promise to cut back on the late-night drinking, which resulted with him remembering more of his dreams the following morning. He simply decided to refrain from following up on any of them, unless they involved people he knew or were major news stories. As much as Ryan wanted to downplay his dream ability, Lisa was still fascinated by it and had other ideas.

She was still obsessed with scanning local news articles about despicable crimes that lacked suspects and continued to create a journal of details for everything she found. What followed was always the same approach with Ryan – dinner, cleanup, TV time with the boys, and alone time with Ryan in the family room to discuss *her list*.

When all of this first started months ago, he was as mystified and excited as Lisa was about what was happening. But over time, Ryan grew tired and stressed out, especially when Sgt. Ramos made his request regarding the Conlin disappearance. Lisa understood, but her curiosity got the better of her and there was just one more request she had been wanting to make. She hoped he would honor one final request that she had been obsessing over, and so she waited until a Friday night where the two could relax, perhaps sip some wine, and discuss it.

Ryan's Friday at work had been uneventful; the usual meetings and the streaming of employees leaving early, hoping to get a jump on the weekend. He was upbeat when he arrived home and instantly welcomed by the aroma of homemade spaghetti sauce on the stove.

Aaron was setting the table. "Hey Dad, wanna watch a Harry Potter movie tonight?"

"Aaron, I'm sure dad's a bit tired," Lisa said while still stirring the sauce. "How about tomorrow night? Besides, there are a few things your father and I need to talk about."

Ryan glared at the back of her head, rolled his eyes, and walked to the bedroom to get changed. *Lisa wanted to talk. Now what?*

After a pleasant dinner, Jason took off to a friend's house down the block while Aaron grabbed a bag of chips and disappeared upstairs to watch his movie. Ryan helped Lisa clear the table and then grabbed his iPhone off the kitchen counter before heading to his La-Z-Boy.

"Can I get you anything before I finish up in here?" Lisa asked, as she finished loading the dishwasher.

"A coffee would be nice. Please." The comment Lisa made to Aaron about *having to talk about a few things tonight* got Ryan thinking, and he decided against the wine. A few minutes later, she carefully carried two freshly brewed cups from the kitchen and set them down on the coffee table. She'd been waiting all week to drop this bombshell on him and the time had come. He was still browsing on his phone when Lisa, leaning back on the sofa, cleared her throat.

"Hon, there's something I've been wanting to ask for a while but have held off because of everything that's gone on with work and Sgt. Ramos. I know I certainly haven't made things any easier for you every time I read up on a crime and ask for you to get involved." Lisa was almost apologetic in her tone, but she now had his full attention. He held the cup to his lips but kept his eyes on her. He knew *something* was coming and braced for it.

"Ryan, I just can't get past what you can do! I mean, to be able to go to sleep and dream yourself to a specific time and place? Think about that for a moment...you can revisit crime scenes and see things that no one else has witnessed!"

"Okay, so where are you going with all of this?" he asked with just a little irritation in his voice.

"Would you be willing to try to go back somewhere if *I* asked you? Somewhere far in the past?" Ryan just stared at her and waited.

"November 1963." She waited for the impact to take effect.

Ryan's look softened, but he still said nothing. Months earlier, they had "lightly" discussed the possibilities regarding historic events but never continued the discussion and instead focused only on helping to solve crimes that could make a difference *now*. And al-though Ryan may have moved on from those historical event discussions, Lisa remained fascinated by them, one in particular. Ryan knew exactly what happened in November 1963.

Neither spoke. Ryan moved his eyes around the room focusing on nothing at all, almost as if to avoid eye contact. Lisa thought he looked overwhelmed, almost shell-shocked.

Finally, he spoke, softly. "And then what?" Before she could answer, Ryan had already begun thinking through it all. "It's been almost sixty years. There have been hundreds of thousands of pages of documents, witness statements, investigations, books written, movies made, and multiple commissions looking at what happened."

"Perhaps. But for every expert panel that said one thing, another expert panel said the opposite. And there's only *one* truth. And we still don't know what that is. Wouldn't you like to know?"

Ryan turned and looked directly at her. "I'll ask you again – and *then* what?" This was stated with a little more conviction. "Ok, let's play the 'what if' game. What if I saw the truth? Who could we tell? We'd just be two more people with opinions on what we thought happened. What if we could unlock all those mysteries of the past? Can you imagine the flood of requests from law enforcement, the general public, and God knows who else? Do you really want to live with that?"

"Perhaps just this one? And we keep it just between us?" she pleaded.

With a deep sigh, Ryan replied with a look of resignation. "Just this one."

# Chapter 47

The dread that Ryan first felt when asked by Lisa to consider the JFK assassination had eased a bit. In fact, he had now become somewhat excited about the idea. For several nights following their discussion, he read dozens of articles online about the assassination, familiarizing himself as best he could about exact locations, timing of events, and eyewitness accounts. He went to sleep each night, never knowing whether or not that would be *the night*.

Every morning, Lisa would wake up early and quietly turn to look at Ryan sleeping. Five days had gone by, and she was as anxious as he seemed to be. And then, early on the sixth morning, everything changed. Lisa was roused from her sleep by a steady rain and an occasional clap of thunder. She turned onto her side to face Ryan, waiting, as she had the past five days, for him to awaken. As the rain continued its rhythmic beat outside, a sudden crack of thunder shook the house. Ryan's eyes opened wide, and he remained motionless, quietly breathing through his open mouth.

"Good morning," Lisa whispered.

Ryan turned his head, his eyes looked distant, and Lisa didn't have to ask, she *knew*. He swallowed hard and began to whisper to her as if the room was bugged. "I was there!" She grabbed his hand with a tight grip.

"It was a sunny day, and I was there in Dealey Plaza in downtown Dallas. Oh my God, Lisa, I was there!" She heard the panic in his voice as if the assassination was happening at that very moment.

Breathing heavily, he continued, "The streets were lined with people. I stood on the sidewalk in front of the Book Depository, and when I turned and looked up, I saw the open window on the 6th floor. It was 12:25, approximately five minutes before the shooting started." Ryan sat up in bed. "I walked toward the grassy knoll where some people were standing, some were sitting. I continued walking to a fence beyond that grassy knoll and leaned against it with a view of the road watching as the president's car appeared. It turned in front of the book depository and came toward me. Just as it approached the spot where I knew he was going to be shot, I turned and saw two figures behind the fence next to me. I heard a distant gunshot and immediately another loud shot from a rifle that appeared between two slats of the fence right next to me. There was chaos everywhere. I turned quickly to see the President's car speed off and when I turned back toward the fence, the two figures were gone."

Lisa laid there hanging on every word. "Oh my God," was all she could said.

"Lisa, I can't unsee what I saw, and I know damn well I'll never forget it. I watched the President get shot. And no one will ever really know." His voice tailed off. Tears welled in his eyes causing Lisa's to do the same.

"Can you take off from work today?" she pleaded.

"Way ahead of you," he said, grabbing his cell phone off the nightstand. While Ryan stayed in bed, Lisa forced herself up to have breakfast with the boys and make sure they got off to school on time. The boys were already at the table when she walked in.

"Mornin' boys, sleep ok?"

Jason was hunched over his notebook, turning pages with one hand while shoving cereal into his mouth with the other. Aaron busied himself reading the back of the cereal box while he ate.

Jason looked up from his notes. "Is dad ok?"

"He's fine," Lisa said. "There's just a lot going on at work and he just needs a day off."

Jason shrugged and continued flipping the pages and finished his breakfast. Lisa sensed that he didn't buy that answer. "OK, Mom, tell dad we hope he feels better. C'mon Aaron, let's get going." The two boys grabbed their backpacks and marched out the side door.

As Lisa paced aimlessly around the kitchen, Ryan emerged from the bedroom. "I overheard what Jason said. I need to spend more time with the boys – and you! Let's sit down this weekend and talk to the boys about going camping."

Over the next two hours, they relived the horror that occurred nearly sixty years earlier. Ryan gave Lisa a moment-by-moment account of everything he "witnessed" from the moment the President's car turned onto Elm Street in Dealey Plaza right up until the shots were fired. The details that he provided were crisp and sure, recalling exactly what people were wearing, where exactly they were standing, and who was using a camera or taking motion pictures.

He recited these details in a somewhat flat, disinterested monotone, but when he got to the details of those two figures behind the fence, the pitch in his voice heightened, his breathing accelerated, and his eyes lit up. *He had seen what some had only speculated about*. He knew that other than satisfying a morbid curiosity, nothing could ever come from this, and he wanted it all to end. He wanted to move on with his life.

# Chapter 48

Agent Mike McShea sat at his desk in FBI Headquarters poring through all the information given to him by agent Henderson about *Jose Ramos Alvarez* and his criminal history. Ramos had remained under the radar for nearly two decades and was, in fact, a stellar cop in the town of Fulton. McShea wondered if perhaps he still might be involved in the drug trade as a small-town cop.

McShea decided that his excuse for calling was to discuss the Jennifer Sears abduction case six months earlier. If there was one thing McShea excelled at, it was interpreting cues about someone from a simple discussion. He placed a blank pad in front of him, reached for the phone, and dialed the Fulton Police Department.

The phone was answered on the first ring, "Fulton Police, how may I help you?"

"This is FBI Agent Mike McShea in our Raleigh office; I'd like to speak with Sgt. Joe Ramos please."

"I'll transfer you now," replied the desk sergeant, who was answering incoming calls because Sarah Bunning was on vacation. Mike McShea imagined the dread that Ramos must have been feeling when he heard that the FBI was calling.

"This is Sgt. Ramos; how may I help you?" The voice was firm, yet friendly, however McShea detected an uncomfortable inflection in the voice that most people wouldn't have picked up on.

"Sgt. Ramos, this is Agent Mike McShea with the FBI. The reason I'm calling is in reference to a child abduction that occurred in Fulton last October. I believe the child's name was Jennifer Sears." McShea stopped talking to study Ramos's response.

"Yes, I'd be glad to send that file over to your office if–"

McShea cut him off. "Would it be possible to discuss this case in person? We're involved in several abduction cases right now and there are a few things I'd like to talk to you about that might benefit a couple of young agents we have working these cases." McShea sounded convincing.

There was a slight delay in the response from Ramos. McShea knew instantly that he had Ramos thinking. "Absolutely, where shall I meet you?" Ramos finally asked.

"Can you swing by the FBI building in Raleigh, say, tomorrow morning at ten?"

"Sure, I'll see you then." Ramos hung up the phone, leaned back in his chair, and stared out the window. He wasn't buying the bit about the young FBI agents learning from the abduction case last October. In all his years on the police force, he never had a call from an FBI agent wanting to meet to discuss a case that was solved months earlier. Ramos felt his heart racing as he entertained the thought of heading home, packing, and disappearing. He rubbed his chin and reasoned that, if the FBI really was after him, they would already be watching and waiting for him to run. He would meet with McShea in the morning.

***

Ramos arrived at the FBI reception desk at precisely 10 a.m. with the Sears abduction folder and was escorted to the office of Mike McShea. The two shook hands, exchanged professional greetings, and sat down opposite each other at the round wooden table in the corner of the office.

"Sgt. Ramos–" McShea started.

"Please, call me Joe," Ramos insisted. "And my gut tells me that there's more to this meeting than what's in this file. Am I right?"

"Okay, Joe. Yes, there's more to it." He saw Ramos getting a little uneasy and sat up in his chair. It's not just the Sears case, it's all of these as well," as McShea tosses a folder across the table at Ramos. "Nine unsolved cases that had few if any leads, and through a series of anonymous tips directed only to you, they are all suddenly solved. Joe, I've been in this business a long time and, well, I've never seen anything quite like it in that short a time span."

Ramos stared at McShea and said nothing. His instincts were on high alert, and they were telling him that McShea was going somewhere with this. McShea soon proved him right and dropped the bomb.

"Joe – or do you still go by the name *Jose*?"

Ramos froze in his seat.

"Listen *Joe*, I know you've got a good reputation over there in Fulton, but you need to come clean with me about whether you're still running a network up here in the States. You work with me, and I'll work with you."

"Wait, you think I'm involved in running drugs into the States?" Ramos asked with amazement. "That stuff was two decades ago. I've been nothing but a clean cop since I got here."

"Well, you didn't exactly come here legally, did you? And all the false documentation? And I'd guess there are some folks south of the border who'd like to see you again. So, what exactly are you into these days, *Mr. Alvarez*?"

Ramos sensed that he was about to be held for what he did in his past and how he came into the country. And it was certainly too late to run. He decided to play his trump card. "You wouldn't believe me if I told you."

McShea looked him in the eye, "Try me."

Over the next two hours, Joe Ramos revealed everything about the tips he got and about Ryan Field. McShea was not convinced with his outrageous tale but nonetheless was intrigued. Although the story about Ryan Field sounded far-fetched, his years of interrogation experience concluded that Ramos was not trying to deceive him.

"I want to meet this guy. In fact, you're going to introduce me to him. And then, you're going to disengage – completely. I'll work with him from here on out. For now, you just remain in Fulton doing what you do."

Ramos nodded.

Agent Jared Henderson was about to enter McShea's office but stopped when he heard the meeting going on. Before walking away, he overheard Ramos speak.

"I'll set up the meeting tomorrow for 1:30 at Pullen Park. We've met there before. I'll tell him it's urgent. We'll be at the benches near the park's entrance." Ramos had promised Ryan that his secret was safe and McShea agreed to keep it that way. Meanwhile, Agent Henderson returned to his desk but kept an eye on McShea's office.

When their meeting ended, McShea escorted Ramos down the hall to the lobby. Agent Henderson briefly glanced up to get a look at the two. He instantly recognized the other guy as Jose Alvarez, the person he was asked by McShea to investigate. He was puzzled as to why they just had a long meeting in McShea's office, why they both left smiling, and now planning to meet tomorrow at 1:30. Henderson felt an uneasy suspicion for McShea. He had uncovered Ramos's hidden criminal past, and now McShea meets with him as if they're friends? Henderson had a thought on how he might confirm his suspicion when McShea returned to his office.

After escorting Ramos out of the building, McShea went back to his office to sift through the notes he had taken, but moments later was interrupted by a knock at the door. "Mike, I've been looking at a few more things regarding that research you had me do. I was wondering if we can discuss it tomorrow. I can reserve the conference room for 1:30." Henderson waited for the response.

"Jared, I've got a doctor's appointment tomorrow at 1:30. How about we make it on Thursday instead?"

"That sounds good. Thursday it is." Agent Henderson turned and walked back to his desk to figure out his next move.

***

Out in the parking lot, Sgt. Ramos sat in his pickup, pulled out his phone, and punched in Ryan's number.

"Mr. Field, this is Sgt. Ramos."

Ryan looked at Lisa and silently mouthed the name of Joe Ramos. "Yes, Sgt. Ramos, how are you this morning?" Ryan asked.

"Mr. Field, would you have time to meet with me tomorrow, I'd–"

"Sgt. Ramos, I've provided you with plenty of information, and I know it's helped your investigations. But that last folder you gave me about one of your own officers, well, look, I don't know if I can do this much longer."

"Please. I'm not asking for any information. There's something I just need to talk to you about," Ramos said with a sense of urgency in his voice.

Ryan agreed to meet the following day, where he would inform Sgt. Ramos that he was through solving crimes. He assured Lisa of his intended conversation and immediately felt a sense of relief.

# Chapter 49

Agent Jared Henderson parked his Honda Civic next to a large pickup truck, which allowed him a clear view of the benches situated near the entrance of Pullen Park. The mild, sun-drenched afternoon welcomed joggers, bike riders, and lunchtime workers to take advantage of Pullen Park's atmosphere. Agent Henderson brought along the props he needed: a newspaper, bag lunch, sunglasses, and of course, his 35mm Nikon. He normally wouldn't have thought much of McShea's investigative business but seeing the friendly banter between McShea and Ramos in the office piqued his interest. And when McShea lied to him about having a doctor's appointment, that just confirmed the suspicion.

Agent Henderson arrived at the park almost one hour before the meeting was planned to take place. He knew that, when meetings are arranged for discreet discussions, people tend to arrive early to "scope out the surroundings." As far as Henderson could tell, he was the first one there.

He reached over and grabbed the newspaper from the passenger seat and the wrapped sandwich he had purchased from a nearby Quik-Mart. With the paper opened against the steering wheel and half a sandwich in one hand, he looked like every other businessman enjoying a quiet lunch hour in the park. His eyes, however, never stopped scanning the park entrance and the benches that were roughly fifty feet in front of him.

At 12:55 p.m., Ryan's Camry entered the park and slowly circled the parking lot before easing into a spot about a dozen spots down from where Agent Henderson was parked. Henderson kept an eye out for McShea and Ramos, but keenly observed every vehicle and park goer in the general vicinity. He did notice one odd thing about the man who had driven up in the silver Camry; he wasn't getting out of his vehicle, didn't appear to be eating his lunch or reading a newspaper, and seemed to be nervously scanning the area.

Every vehicle entering the park came under the watchful eye of agent Henderson. At 1:15 p.m., a white pickup truck caught his attention when it slowly drove around the lot twice before coming to rest at the far end of the parking lot under a tree. A short, stocky man in a baseball cap got out and walked directly to the benches where the entrance road meets the parking lot. Agent Henderson recognized him immediately.

Sgt. Ramos, dressed in jeans and polo shirt, took a seat on the bench, leaned back, and clasped his hands in front of him. From the corner of his eye, Henderson saw the figure in the Camry get out of his vehicle, walk across the parking lot, and take a seat on the bench next to Sgt. Ramos. As the two engaged in conversation, Henderson retrieved his camera from its case, attached a zoom lens, and began quietly snapping pictures, focusing primarily on the fellow next to Ramos.

"Sgt. Ramos, before you tell me what was so urgent about this meeting, I'd like to say something. I'm tired. I'm glad I've been able to help, but no more. This has affected my health, my job, and my family life. You said you wanted to meet and *not* ask for any kind of information. So, what is it you want?" Ryan saw that Sgt. Ramos appeared a bit uncomfortable.

Off to the side, a figure walking along the path approached the pair and stopped in front of them. Ryan was surprised when the stranger sat down next to Sgt. Ramos without saying a word. Henderson's camera never stopped as McShea joined the group.

"Ryan, this is agent Mike McShea with the FBI," Ramos said quietly.

Ryan looked to be in a state of shock. "What the hell is this all about? Are you kidding me?"

"I'm sorry Ryan." Sgt. Joe Ramos looked and sounded helpless. "Agent McShea is going to be your point of contact from here on. Again, I'm sorry." Ramos stood up, and without acknowledging either one, walked to his pickup at the far end of the parking lot, got in, and drove away.

Walking out on Ryan Field that way was against everything Sgt. Joe Ramos stood for. He had spent years in the community working to build trusting relationships with everyone he met. But now, his career and his life were on the line and there was no way he could tell Ryan he was being blackmailed by an FBI agent.

"Mr. Field, I know this isn't what you expected at this meeting, but there are reasons why Sgt. Ramos must have no further involvement," McShea said.

"So, what exactly has Ramos told you?" Ryan probed.

"He informed me of how you've helped him in the past with some unusual ability you claim to have. You must understand how odd it appeared that one particular sergeant from a small-town police department suddenly began to solve crimes through anonymous tips. He felt it was in his best interest to confide in me and that's where we are now." McShea didn't elaborate any further.

"Look," Ryan began, "I'll tell you what I told Sgt. Ramos. I can't do this anymore. I don't *want* to do this anymore. My health has suffered, and it's affected both my job and my family life. I hope he at least mentioned that to you."

"I understand," McShea said sympathetically. "You certainly sound like you need a break from this. But I would like for us to stay in touch," as he handed Ryan his business card.

The two stood up, shook hands and parted ways. Ryan knew that those final words about *staying in touch* was McShea's way of saying he's going to want something down the road. As Ryan got into his vehicle and drove off, Agent Henderson took one last picture to capture the Camry's license plate

# Chapter 50

Sgt. Joe Ramos had quietly resumed his local police duties and made every effort to keep a low profile and avoid any interaction with Ryan and Lisa. Agent Jared Henderson became involved in other assignments and rarely worked with Mike McShea anymore, although every now and then he'd open that Ramos folder he kept in his desk and wonder why the interest in it had died down. One day he walked by McShea in the hallway and stopped to question him about it. McShea seemed to brush it off and told him that *he was just assisting Sgt. Ramos in an old investigation that's still ongoing.* Agent Henderson accepted McShea's explanation and moved on. Just the same, he kept that folder in a safe place. *What about Ramos's past?*

***

Two months had passed since the meeting in Pullen Park and Ryan's introduction to Mike McShea. Ryan hadn't heard from anyone since that day and hoped he had fallen off McShea's radar. He didn't miss the intrusions and stress that took its toll on him at home and at work. And although he continued to have dreams about random crimes, he chose not to follow up on them, and they'd soon be forgotten. Lisa also refrained from her own crusade of researching local crimes and thankfully ceased from pressuring Ryan with any more of her "requests."

In the two months since meeting Ryan, Agent McShea kept more to himself, often worked behind a closed office door, and did just enough at his job to keep his boss happy. His interest turned to the yacht hanging on his wall and daydreaming about life after the FBI. He had an idea and thought perhaps it was time to give Ryan Field a call.

Ryan was the last to leave the conference room after participating in a healthy discussion about a recommendation he submitted to increase ridership on the proposed rail system. He was pleased at how well it was accepted by management and was strutting down the hall when he felt the vibration of his cell phone in his pocket signaling a call. He pulled it out but didn't immediately recognize the number.

"Hello?" he said in a cautious tone.

"Mr. Field? Mike McShea here."

Ryan hurried into his office and closed the door. "Agent McShea, been awhile, what can I do for you?" Ryan said not really wanting to hear the answer.

"Ryan, I could use your assistance. I promise, this is just between you and me. There's an Exxon station at the light one block west of your office building. Are you familiar with it?"

Ryan rolled his eyes and shook his head, not wanting to believe McShea had called him asking for *assistance*. "Yes, I know where it is," he replied flatly.

"Good, I'll be there at 5 p.m. tonight, it won't take long." McShea hung up.

Ryan left his office at 4:55 p.m. and took his time walking to his car. Three minutes later he turned his car into the Exon station where he noticed McShea's car parked off to the side. The silver Camry eased to a stop behind McShea's car, but before he could get out, McShea jumped out and approached him with a large envelope in his hand. Ryan remained in his car and lowered the window.

"Ryan, good to see you again. I could really use your help with this. Can you take a look and call me if you have any questions?" McShea did his best to sound sincere.

Ryan felt the stress coming back. "It's been a while, but I'll see what I can do."

McShea nodded then walked to his car.

Ryan tossed the envelope onto the passenger seat and drove

home. He wore a different look on his face when he arrived home that night, one that Lisa hadn't seen in a couple of months. "I had a visitor today. Remember my good friend Agent McShea?" he said with obvious sarcasm. Lisa recognized the name and saw the envelope in Ryan's hand.

"Oh no! Any idea what it's about?" Lisa asked sympathetically.

"He didn't say, just handed me this and said to contact him if I had any questions," he responded in a somewhat deflated tone. "It's been two months. I don't even know if I'm able to do it anymore! Sorry hon, I'm not real hungry tonight. I just need to take a look at this." He walked to his office without bothering to make a detour to change out of his work clothes.

Ryan pulled out several pages from the envelope and noticed that none of them were stamped or had any indicators relating to the FBI or any government agency. The paper was plain, and the typed text was ordinary and very unofficial looking. The first few paragraphs described a bank heist that occurred in Gastonia, North Carolina. It included the location of the bank, the date, and the exact time of the crime. There were other details that Ryan skimmed over about the town, history of the bank, and bank personnel. At the bottom of the last page, McShea provided his handwritten request – *please note the vehicle used in the getaway*. Ryan thought this was a rather simple request, considering what he had been able to do in the past.

Lisa was surprised to see Ryan emerge from his office after only ten minutes and appearing calm. He knew she was anxiously waiting for him to tell her what it was about, even as she pretended not to notice he had entered the kitchen.

"A bank robbery in Gastonia. He wants me to identify the getaway car," Ryan told her.

"Are you ok with that?"

"Sure. I'll try and we'll just see what happens. I'm just hoping he doesn't make a habit of this."

***

Mike McShea sat at his kitchen table finishing up the remainder of his Chinese take-out from the previous evening and washed it down with a cold Budweiser. Next to his plate lay an open folder with details of a bank robbery in Gastonia several months earlier. He had given all the information to Ryan *except* the make, model, and color of the getaway car. That information was never made public, and the only way Ryan could correctly tell him what it is, would be to revisit the day of the crime and see for himself. Then, he would be convinced Ryan could do what he and Sgt. Ramos claims he can do.

Agent McShea thought that his request was a simple one and was surprised he hadn't heard back from Ryan the next day. The morning after, however, his cell phone buzzed at 8:45 and Ryan Field's name and number lit up the screen. "Mr. Field?"

"Agent McShea, I have what you're looking for. Red Hyundai Elantra. Maybe a 2013 or 14, license plate number TRN1422" Ryan said proudly.

"That's great, I really appreciate your help. I'll be in touch." McShea hung up. Ryan had passed the test.

# Chapter 51

Agent Mike McShea's successful dry run with Ryan Field and the Gastonia bank robbery boosted his confidence in Ryan's ability to visit past crime scenes. McShea spent every night over the following several weeks pouring through a database containing FBI files of unsolved crimes, specifically, crimes where large sums of cash went missing and never recovered. Most of these cases involved bank robberies, something McShea wanted to avoid since banks are known to include marked bills during a robbery to make it easier to identify stolen cash. Instead, he set his sights on the drug dealers, not the street hustlers, but the suppliers. And there was a name that came to mind who was rumored to be a major player in the Raleigh area – Alberto Cerrone.

Known by the name *Berto*, Cerrone had worked his way up in the drug business since arriving from Miami in early 2003. He was always smart enough not to get his hands dirty or be anywhere near a drug transaction. Every time he was dragged into a courtroom, regardless of the charges, he would be accompanied by some of the best defense attorneys in the state, always resulting with him walking out of court a free man. He lived in a lavish home in the North Hills section north of Raleigh, owned a fleet of exotic cars, and was known to donate large sums of money into the local community and its politicians.

Berto was a night owl who would often be seen at a specific night club he frequented in the downtown Raleigh district. McShea was convinced Berto did much of his business with contacts who frequented the club. Despite being raided in the past resulting with a few locals getting busted on possession, nothing major was ever found. Berto's house, however, with the steady stream of late-night visitors, was another story. It was located at the end of a cul-de-sac in one of the most luxurious parts of town, with a large stone wall lining the property's perimeter ensuring that curious eyes got nothing to look at. The more McShea investigated Alberto Cerrone, the more intrigued he became.

Ryan was humming along to Elton John's *Crocodile Rock* on the drive to Home Depot on Saturday morning to pick up a few gallons of paint for the family room. The song was suddenly interrupted by an incoming call through the car's Bluetooth. He reached over and tapped the display to answer the call.

"Hello?" he shouted.

"Ryan – this is Mike, Mike McShea." Ryan silently mouthed an expletive as McShea continued. "Ryan, I wouldn't be bothering you unless it was vitally important – and involved something extremely harmful to our community." He let those words linger for a moment.

Ryan pulled into the Home Depot parking lot and parked in a vacant spot at the end of the lot. "I'm listening," was all he said.

"There's someone local that we believe is a major player in the drug business – and he's right here in the area. We haven't been able to get close to this guy, and every time he's dragged into court, his team of lawyers have him walking right out."

Ryan turned off the Bluetooth connection and held his cell phone to his ear. "So, what is it you want me to do?"

"Basically, do the surveillance that we're not able to do. Ryan, apparently, you've got a capability we simply don't have. Would you be able to meet for a few minutes today? I can provide you with the details at that time." McShea had all the specific details written down and the instructions for Ryan to follow.

Ryan was intrigued by the request but didn't want Lisa to know about this until he knew the details. "If it won't take long, how about we meet now? I just have to run into Home Depot and pick a few things up. Then I can meet you."

McShea agreed to meet Ryan there at Home Depot, and in the time it took for Ryan to purchase what he needed, McShea would be rolling into the parking lot. Ryan walked out into the bright sunlight to his car at the far end of the lot. After placing his items in the trunk, he got in just as McShea slowly pulled up next to him.

They both lowered their windows and, after a friendly nod, McShea reached out and gave Ryan a large envelope. Ryan immediately opened it and viewed its contents. After a moment, he looked over at McShea, "Okay, let's talk about this a minute. You want me in this guy's house at 2 a.m. every night over a two-week period? For what exactly?"

"Ryan, this guy claims to manage a car dealership for a living, but once you see how he lives, you'll know something doesn't add up. Why 2 a.m.? Because he has a night routine. Two or three days a week he's out in the clubs downtown, one in particular, and returns home around that time. If we could get some absolute assurance that he's hiding a supply of drugs and cash in his home, then we can move in on him – and this time make it stick in court!"

Although Ryan told Lisa he was getting tired of the demands by Ramos and was annoyed by McShea, this request piqued his interest because of what was involved. He gave McShea a nod, rolled up his window, and drove off. Painting the family room was the last thing on his mind as he wound through the side streets near his home. He decided he wasn't going to tell Lisa about the meeting with McShea, at least not yet.

# Chapter 52

"You're awfully quiet tonight, feeling okay?" Lisa asked, as she removed her robe and slid into bed. She also noticed that the novel he had been engrossed in for the past several nights remained undisturbed on the nightstand.

"Just a long day of painting, I guess," was all Ryan could come up with. Thinking she might recognize this behavior from his Joe Ramos days, he quickly changed the subject. "Hey, I know - how about tomorrow morning I make everyone my famous Belgian waffles?"

"It's a deal!" Lisa gave him a kiss, turned over, and reached to turn out the light.

Ryan turned on his side facing away from her. For the past hour, he had thought of nothing except the details that McShea gave him about Alberto Cerrone. He closed his eyes and allowed the quiet hum of the air conditioner to lull him to sleep.

*The North Hills estate was opulent. Tall metal gates opened to a long, winding driveway lined with finely cut granite stones. Accent lighting glowed at the base of trees and perfectly trimmed hedges. He could hear the muffled sound of a bass-heavy Latin beat coming from inside the house as some partygoers gathered in small groups scattered on the property.*

*Inside, the thumping beat of the music resonated in every room. Men dressed in silk shirts sporting gold chains cruised through the house as glamourous women in tight skirts, revealing tops, and loads of diamonds competed to be noticed. This was a world Ryan had never seen and really wanted no part of. And although the drugs and alcohol flowed freely among the guests, 'Berto" Cerrone seemed to stay far from it, instead, walking around ensuring that his guests had what they needed. Ryan drifted around, but never veered far from Berto, always keeping him in sight. The only exception was the frequent trips Berto would take to a back room down thc hall from the main parlor. Ryan took a few steps toward the hallway, but everything began to fade away.*

Ryan woke to the sound of the toilet flushing. He tried to focus his eyes as Lisa emerged from the bathroom in her pink bathrobe and sat down on his side of the bed. "You know what time it is?" she asked in a deadpan voice. "Belgian waffle time! I've been thinking about that ever since I woke up this morning!"

He stared at her as his thoughts slipped back to the dream he just had. He had to quickly drop that thought. "Do me a favor? Can you make some of your famous coffee, and I'll be right out to whip us up some of my famous waffles?"

"You bet!" she said and walked to the kitchen.

Ryan laid there for a moment and closed his eyes to revisit an image of the house and party guests he had just seen. There really wasn't much to it, other than a decadent party and frequent trips to a mysterious room at the end of the hall, but he'd give Mike McShea a call just the same. First, he had an appointment in the kitchen he had to keep.

By 9 a.m., everyone had finished their special breakfast, and the boys returned upstairs while Lisa and Ryan sat nursing a second cup of Lisa's special brew. "The family room looks great," Lisa said admiring the paint job. "I'll help you move all the furniture back in place after we finish up here."

"Thanks, that room was sure overdue!" Ryan kept up the conversation's enthusiasm, not wanting to take a chance that Lisa might suspect Ryan's mind was elsewhere. "I need to make another trip to Home Depot sometime today. I messed up a little around the window frame and need to do some touch up. Nothing major."

***

Mike McShea never had an issue with getting calls on the

weekend. So, when his phone rang at 10:45 Sunday morning, he was excited to see the caller ID come up as *Ryan Field*.

"Ryan, good morning," McShea answered in an uncharacteristically friendly tone.

"Hello Mike. Just wanna follow up with you. I paid a visit to our friend's house last night."

"Helluva spread, isn't it?" McShea joked.

"Oh yeah. Quite a party going on there. Not sure I can tell you anything you don't already know. A lot of fancy individuals doing a lot of drugs and alcohol. Nothing else too obvious except...our friend didn't appear to partake in any of the 'refreshments' but did make frequent trips to a back room."

"And?" McShea was hanging on every word.

"Sorry, but that was as far as I got. Nights just aren't as long as they used to be," Ryan said lightly. "Perhaps another time."

"If you could, that would be great. Anything else you could find would really help. If we could just catch him in possession of a large drug supply and cash, we'd make our move. He always seems to be one step ahead of us though."

"I'll be in touch." Ryan hung up, as he exited his Camry and walked toward the entrance of Home Depot. It felt good to be the one to end the call and hang up.

# Chapter 53

The emotional roller coaster that Ryan had lived since discovering his dream ability took another turn when McShea approached him with the file on Alberto Cerrone. Ryan was euphoric when he heard the news that his dreams led to finding little Jennifer Sears months ago. The enthusiasm waned, however, as more and more requests were made by Joe Ramos and his wife. He started to lose focus with his job and his family, and when McShea thrusted himself into the picture, that was the last straw. But, after a quiet couple of months, McShea re-established contact and once he got involved in the Cerrone case, the feeling of excitement returned.

Over the next ten days following his first visit to Berto's house, Ryan was able to visit several more times. Being an *observer*, he couldn't actively *do* anything, so if Berto wasn't home or was already asleep, it was basically a wasted night. Then, on Ryan's fourth 2 a.m. visit, he found himself standing in the main parlor in the company of three men.

*Berto sat on the edge of the leather couch facing the other two who were sitting comfortably in matching leather chairs. Between them was a glass table upon which there was a large zip lock bag of white powder resting near two glasses of Scotch and a third glass of tonic water. Leaning up against the table on the side of the two men was a briefcase. Ryan stood just a few feet away, mesmerized by what he was seeing.*

*After several minutes of random conversation and light laughter, one of the two visitors reached down and lifted the black leather briefcase onto the table, dialed in the numbers to unlock the latches, and opened it so it faced Berto. Ryan was positioned to have a clear view of the rows of stacked bills that filled the case. The stacks were removed, placed on the table, and replaced in the briefcase with the large bag of white powder. Berto placed the cash into a small gym bag and placed the bag on the couch next to him. He then called out for two nearby associates to escort the visitors to the front door. The large brass wall clock read 2:45.*

*Ryan watched as Berto picked up the gym bag and turned to walk to that back room down the hall, the one he had made so many frequent trips to during that party Ryan witnessed the previous week. Ryan followed him into the room, which contained a huge mahogany desk and walls lined with filled bookcases. He looked around, doubting that Berto had ever read a single book in the room. Berto still clutched the gym bag full of cash and walked to the far corner of the room, dropped the bag, and removed a book from a shelf that was about five feet above floor level. Reaching his hand into the vacated spot, he paused a moment, then with his free hand, effortlessly swung the bookcase open as if it was a revolving door, revealing a huge safe.*

*Ryan got a little closer as Berto spun the tumblers in both directions until he heard the click indicating it was unlocked. He pulled on the heavy, thick door until it was opened as far as it could go. As Berto reached down to retrieve the cash from the gym bag, Ryan peered over his shoulder and gasped at the contents of the safe. The stacks that were being added paled in comparison to what was in there already, in addition to numerous Ziplock bags of white powder similar to what the visitors had left with tonight.*

Ryan faded away from this room and opened his eyes to Lisa lying next to him.

# Chapter 54

Mike McShea hung on every word about Ryan's experience the night before. When Ryan described the safe and its contents, he couldn't help himself, and threw a fist pump into the air. His assumption that Berto was dealing from his home was proven correct. His plan was now in motion.

"Okay, so let's go over this one more time. This office with the bookshelves – this is at the end of the long hallway on the left as you leave the parlor?" McShea asked as he frantically scribbled on a small notepad.

"Yep. After you enter the office, there's a bookshelf straight ahead. On the left side, third shelf from the top, there's a thick blue book. You can't miss it. Pull this book out, reach in, and there must be a button or latch or something to press, because once his hand was in there, he was easily able to rotate the bookshelf open like a revolving door!" There was a hint of excitement in Ryan's voice.

"And the safe?" McShea asked.

"It's huge. Must be about six feet high, four feet wide, and weigh a ton!" Ryan gushed. "I stood right there as he opened it – twenty-two right, two turns left stopping at seven, one turn right past seven stopping at fifteen, then left to thirty-three."

"Got it. Ryan, you've confirmed what we had believed but could never be sure of," McShea said. "I can't thank you enough for what you've done. Of course, I 'll keep all of this confidential between us. I'll make sure you always remain anonymous."

The call ended and Mike McShea sat in the silence of his living room staring at his note pad. He placed it into his briefcase for safekeeping. Leaning back and shutting his eyes, he pictured the interior of Berto's house as Ryan explained it; the parlor, hallway leading to the office, the bookshelves, and that big, black, beautiful safe.

Over the course of the previous several weeks, Mike McShea had performed his own surveillance of Alberto Cerrone, tracking his movements throughout Raleigh, taking note of when he arrived at his usual club, when he left, and where and when he stopped to eat. Of all the nights, Wednesday night was the most predictable. Berto would leave his home between 9 and 10 p.m., drive the same route to the Apollo Club, have the valet park his car, then sit in the same VIP area at the back of the club. When the club would close at 1 a.m., he would usually stay and talk with the club's owner for no more than thirty minutes before heading home. At that late hour, Berto always chose to use the quiet back roads to his North Hills estate and was always a quick drive with little, if any, traffic.

# Chapter 55

A cold front blew in the following Wednesday bringing with it a steady light rain which began just before noon. McShea spent most of the day shuttered in his office consumed with details for what he had planned out for the rest of the night. He arrived home by 6 o'clock, made himself a turkey sandwich, and got comfortable in front of the TV intending to watch the news. Instead, he watched the clock.

At 8:30 p.m., Mike McShea strolled out of his apartment and drove downtown, parked on a dark side street, then walked in the drizzly rain to the Barnes & Noble bookstore that didn't close until ten. There, he purchased a bottle of water, picked a random novel from a display table, and sat near a window near the front with an unobstructed view of the Apollo nightclub entrance. The weather helped by persuading many of the Wednesday night crowd to remain home. McShea occasionally glanced down and randomly turned pages of the novel, however, his full attention was on the club's entrance, specifically, cars that would stop and linger in front of the club.

The crowd in the bookstore had thinned since McShea arrived and the tables around him soon were empty and being wiped down by an employee. Another glance up, he spied a black, late model Mercedes slowly rolling to a stop across the street at 9:25 p.m. The club's parking attendant quickly ran around the back of the car to the driver's door, arriving at the same time the door began to open. Opening an umbrella, the attendant walked alongside Alberto Cerrone until he was under the canopy at the front door. As Berto disappeared into the club, the attendant ran back and jumped into the driver's seat. McShea got up and returned the novel to the display table nearby and returned to his car.

With the knowledge that Alberto Cerrone was at the Apollo club as expected, Mike McShea left the downtown area and drove the backroads to the North Hills area, a route he had driven numerous times and became quite familiar with. He had done his homework. McShea familiarized himself with all of the properties that bordered the home of Alberto Cerrone, on his street and behind his home, taking note of which homeowners had dogs. His sedan entered the North Hills community at roughly 9:45 p.m., and the falling rain had stopped.

A bike path and wooded areas bordered the northwest corner of Alberto Cerrone's property in the back. McShea parked his car on a quiet street two blocks away and walked along the bike path until he reached a row of thick hedges protecting a short wrought-iron fence to access Cerrone's property. The only lighting in the backyard was the bright blue glow of the swimming pool. McShea was able to approach along the side of the property staying within the shadows almost up until he reached the side of the house. He was fully aware of the elaborate security system Alberto Cerrone had installed and how to circumvent it. Nine months earlier, an FBI team disguised as a city utility crew was able to access the property to update utility meters in the neighborhood. During the ruse, the team studied the security system in place and developed a method to deactivate it if it ever became necessary. McShea had studied that particular FBI file and knew exactly what to do. The outside connection box was exactly where it had been identified in the file and once he had located it and broken off the lock, he was easily able to disconnect the security system.

Mike McShea deftly picked the lock and entered through the back door to a large room that featured floor to ceiling windows overlooking the pool. He cautiously navigated his way to the main parlor that Ryan spoke of and the long hallway with the room at the far end on the left. The hallway contained a long runway of carpet that absorbed any sounds McShea may have made making his way down the hall. With a small, thin-beamed flashlight in one hand, he used his other to slowly open the door and enter the back office. McShea was amazed at the accuracy at what Ryan had told him. The bookcase and the thick blue book were exactly as he had described them. He carefully gripped the blue book and after sliding it out, set it down on the floor. He aimed the flashlight's thin beam into the area vacated by the book, and at the back was a small red button. When he reached in and pressed the button, the entire bookcase moved slightly and with his other hand, he was able to effortlessly rotate it open, revealing the huge safe.

McShea wasted little time as his gloved hand gripped the dial - Twenty-two right, two turns left stopping at seven, one turn right past seven stopping at fifteen, then left to thirty-three. He grabbed the handle and gave it a twist. The solid door opened smoothly, revealing several shelves, closed compartments, and a large open area at the bottom filled with stacks of wrapped cash. McShea straightened and took a deep breath, awed by the sight in front of him. He looked at his watch - 10:55. Reaching into his pocket, he pulled out a folded nylon bag, snapped it open, and began filling it until the bottom of the safe was empty. He then opened each closed compartment, finding over a dozen large Ziploc bags of white powder in some, and assorted jewelry and gems in another. He closed the compartments leaving the contents undisturbed.

Once the safe door had been shut, he slowly rotated the bookcase back to its original position and replaced the blue book back onto the shelf. He picked up the bag, and walked to the hallway, glancing around to ensure nothing had been disturbed. He continued this routine as he walked through the parlor and out the back. Voices. McShea heard what sounded like a conversation between a man and woman coming from the path behind the house. He froze with his back up against the side of the house gripping the nylon bag. The voices continued but soon became weaker in the moments that followed. Just a couple out for a late-night stroll, he concluded. He quickly reactivated the security system and crept quietly back to the hedges where he scaled the short fence and squeezed through to the wooded area and bike path. McShea was careful to leave the premises exactly as he had found them, with one glaring exception – the safe's contents. He walked in the darkness along the path, emerging two blocks from his car. The time was 11:25. Mike McShea arrived at his car, confident that he hadn't been seen by anyone and hearing only the distant bark of a dog from a block over. He threw the bag in the trunk of his car, covered it, and casually drove off to complete the next step of tonight's plan.

The back roads from the Apollo nightclub to Alberto Cerrone's estate were dark, curvy, and travelled primarily by local residents. Mike McShea had scouted this route carefully to find just the right area off the road where he could park unnoticed to passing traffic. He arrived at the half-hidden spot off the side of the road near midnight and turned off his engine. Several cars passed by McShea's position over the next two hours, none matching the description of the car he was waiting for.

McShea glanced at his watch and took several deep breaths to relax. The car he was expecting to pass by could come at any moment. Twenty minutes passed and then the darkness was interrupted by two faint beams of light approaching. As the car cruised by him, McShea recognized it as Berto's black Mercedes. He waited until the car disappeared around a curve, then pulled out onto the two-lane road in pursuit. When McShea had the Mercedes tail lights in his sight, he sped up and flipped on his flashing blue lights. Without hesitation, the black Mercedes pulled over onto the gravel and rolled to a stop.

Berto turned off the engine and eyed McShea in his side view mirror as he exited his vehicle. McShea's badge was clearly visible on his hip and the flashlight he carried was trained on the driver side window. A loaded 9-mm Glock rested under Berto's seat, as he positioned both hands on the steering wheel. "Can you tell me what the issue is officer?" Berto politely asked.

"Do you live in this area?" McShea asked with a tone of authority.

"About three miles from here in North Hills Estates."

"May I see your license and registration please? There was a car broken into in the area about an hour ago ,and we're checking everyone on the road right now," McShea said.

Berto seemed relieved. "Of course, officer," and he reached over to the glove compartment for the registration. The moment Berto turned to open the glove compartment, McShea pulled out his .38 revolver and fired three shots. As Alberto Cerrone's lifeless body slumped across the console, McShea calmly walked back to his car.

# Chapter 56

Mike McShea drove off down the dark, two-lane road leaving a grisly scene behind him. He didn't encounter another vehicle until he hit the main highway, and at that late hour, there were few. Approximately a mile before reaching his apartment complex, he stopped off at an all-night convenience store to pick up a loaf of bread and a few other odds and ends. While at the counter, he looked up and observed the lone security camera hanging limp, wrapped in gray duct tape. This eased his concern of being caught on surveillance. He walked out carrying the large bag of items and placed them in the trunk of his car. Before closing the trunk, he removed the items from the grocery bag and replaced them with the nylon bag of money.

Several minutes later, he arrived at his apartment complex and pulled into the parking garage under the watchful eye of the building's security camera. Opening the trunk, he removed his bag of "groceries" and entered the building. McShea shut and locked the door behind him, tossed the bag on the couch, and let out a huge exhale. He was not a frequent drinker, but that night was an exception, and he celebrated the night's feat with an ice-filled glass of Scotch.

The contents of the nylon bag spilled out and created a mound of wrapped currency on the cushion by his side. One-by-one he counted the stacks and then placed them back into the nylon bag. Most of the bundles were of $100 bills, however, there were bundles of twenties mixed in. The final tally of $155,000 was taken back to the bedroom and hidden deep within the closet. Exhausted and feeling the effects of the Scotch, he removed his clothes and fell into bed, but not before setting his alarm for eight o'clock so he could call in sick.

***

Having slept barely four hours, McShea was abruptly woken and strained to open his eyes. His head was pounding from the Scotch as he reached for the phone to call Jared Henderson.

"Jared, Mike McShea here," he said in a raspy, coarse voice. "I won't be in today, trying to fight off whatever it is I've got."

"Hey Mike, yeah, you don't sound so good. I'll let anyone looking for you that you'll be out today."

"Thanks Jared. Hopefully, I'll be in tomorrow," and the call ended.

McShea poured himself a large glass of water and took three aspirin. He dragged himself to the couch, grabbed the remote, and tuned in to the local news. After several national stories were reported, the day's local breaking news stories were next. McShea's ears perked when he heard what he was waiting for: "A suspected drug dealer with a long criminal history was found killed in an apparent gangland slaying last night on a quiet road in North Raleigh. No suspects or eye-witnesses at this time." He anticipated that when the police searched the home of Alberto Cerrone, they would find the safe and its cache of drugs and stolen jewelry. He was sure that they would do some obligatory investigation and soon the case of Alberto Cerrone would die down and fade away with one more local bad guy removed from society. Mike McShea leaned back, put his feet up on the table, and clasped his hands behind his head, quite pleased with himself.

# Chapter 57

The manager's impromptu meeting called at the end of the workday on Thursday caught Ryan and the entire staff off guard. The conference room filled with tense faces and cautious murmuring waited for Program Manager Jim Asom to make his appearance. Transportation projects, especially large rail projects like this, were often favorite targets of politicians looking to trim budgets. Joe Farrell planted himself next to Ryan against the wall.

"What do ya think, we got maybe six months left on this job?" Farrell said with a wry grin. "How 'bout we buy a piece of land and open up a drive-in movie theater?"

Ryan looked at Farrell and rolled his eyes. "What a great idea!" he said with as much sarcasm as he could muster. The random conversations came to a halt as Jim Asom entered and stood at the front of the room.

Asom cleared his throat. "I'll try to be brief. There's been much concern recently about the future of our project here. I'd like to tell you that this morning I received a call from corporate, and we've secured the funding required to finish out the project." Mass exhaling and elated whispers filled the room. "Having said that, let's head back to work and finish what we started without that dark cloud hanging over us."

After five more minutes of telling everyone what a great job they were doing, Asom left the conference room. As everyone else got up to leave, Ryan looked at Joe Farrell and shook his head. "Ya know, I was really getting excited about that drive-in movie idea!" The workday passed quickly after that, and Ryan couldn't wait to get home and share the good news.

"Hey Dad!" Jason shouted from the garage, as the Camry rolled up the driveway. "Mom got pizza from Gino's!"

Ryan could smell the aroma the moment he opened the door to the kitchen. "Come here, you," he said as he grabbed Lisa and pulled her into his arms. "Good news – Asom spoke to us today and said we're fully funded!"

"Oh, hon, that's great! Sorry, I didn't feel like cooking tonight," she said apologetically.

"Are you kidding? Today's news, Gino's pizza, and all of us together is all I need right now! How about a glass of red to celebrate?"

Lisa placed the large pizza box on the table and watched as it was assaulted by all her men at the table. Once everyone settled into their seats, the table chatter started with Ryan's day at work, followed by stories of the boys' day in school and the neighborhood gossip Lisa had heard on her walk with the neighbor next door. After forty-five minutes, all that was left was an empty pizza box, a pile of crumpled napkins, and a couple of empty wine glasses. The boys disappeared, and Ryan left to get changed.

"Can I get you a refill?" Lisa asked Ryan as he returned to the kitchen.

"Just half, please, it's been a day!" Ryan detoured into the family room and into his favorite chair, soon joined by Lisa. Instinctively, he reached for the remote and turned on the local news; a dog rescued from a ravine, a fire that destroyed part of the town's public library, and a three-car accident backed up a nearby highway for several hours. What Ryan heard next though, grabbed his attention: "Raleigh Police are investigating the killing of suspected drug dealer Alberto Cerrone late last night several miles from his home in North Raleigh. No other details at this time."

"What's up?" Lisa asked when she noticed Ryan's expression suddenly change. He hadn't said a word to Lisa about what he had done for Mike McShea, but Lisa was quick to recognize the change in his demeanor when that story was announced. She'd seen it before.

"Remember that FBI agent I helped out with that robbery in Gastonia? Well, there was a second request, and I really didn't want to concern you with it."

"A request for what?"

"That killing they just reported on. Alberto Cerrone? It had to do with him," Ryan confessed, not going into any further details. "Look, it's over now. He was a bad dude, and now he's gone. It's over."

Lisa stood up without looking at him and walked toward the kitchen, stopped and turned around. "You know, you really don't have to hide anything from me. I've supported you with this from the very beginning."

"I know, I'm sorry. I just didn't want to burden you with it, and I was really trying to distance myself from these requests altogether. I'm confident that this should be the end of it." Ryan didn't dare mention to Lisa that spying around the home of a drug kingpin had excited him.

# Chapter 58

Ten months earlier in a small town on the outskirts of Charlotte, Alvin Bradford, a part-time carpenter and petty thief, parked his car on a secluded street late one night and slithered several blocks through an old neighborhood in search of an *opportunity*. He came upon a large, wooded park which hosted ballgames and young families during the day but sat eerily silent once the sun set, except for the occasional teenage couple rolling around under a blanket. Alvin, packing a small .22 caliber handgun in his belt, proceeded into the park, followed the path but walked off to the side on flattened grass. He continued walking away from the path and into a lightly wooded area, stopping when he heard voices a short distance in front of him.

Alvin quietly advanced, making sure there was always a tree between him and the voices coming from beyond the trees. When he could go no further without being seen, he stopped and hid behind a thick oak tree to peer around its side and observe two figures, perhaps thirty feet away, standing near a bench. Alvin was unable to hear their conversation but did notice each was clutching a briefcase. One of the figures, who was tall and on the lean side, rested his briefcase on the bench then unlocked and opened it up to reveal its contents. The second, thickly built figure leaned over, ran his fingers through it, then brought them to his mouth. After a moment and brief exchange, the second figure opened his briefcase on the bench while the first figure closed his and turned on a flashlight.

Alvin's eyes grew wide, and he tried not to blink or breathe too heavily. He repositioned slightly against the tree, and in doing so, stepped on a small dry twig. The distinct snapping sound caused both heads to suddenly turn his way. Alvin froze, moving his right hand to his waistband and resting it on the handle of his gun. Then, as he watched, one of the figures reached into his pocket, pulled out a firearm, and shot the other who was holding the flashlight.

This was not the first time Vic Santoro had arranged a meeting in this park with his unnamed dealer, but just the same, he didn't trust him. He was high and a little paranoid, and when he heard that sudden noise coming from behind a nearby tree, he sensed he was being set-up. After shooting the dealer, he turned and walked toward the trees from where that sound had come, pointing his gun with his arm extended fully in front of him. Alvin, still ducking behind the tree, eased the .22 from his waistband and readied himself. Vic Santoro walked toward the tree near the one Alvin was hiding behind and when he was just a few feet away, Alvin lunged out and shot twice. The first shot struck Santoro in the upper chest; the second shot hit him in the neck, causing him to fall backward and hit the ground with a loud thud, dropping both his gun and the briefcase he was holding. Alvin quickly picked up the briefcase and opened it revealing stacks of hundred-dollar bills.

Alvin thrust the gun back in his waistband and ran toward the other lifeless figure by the bench and opened the briefcase that was lying next to the body. Inside were large bags of white powder, one of which was slightly opened. He quickly shut it and left it where it was. He could use the cash but wanted no part of the drugs. The gunshots echoed in the night, and he was sure the police would soon be on their way. With the briefcase of cash firmly in his grip, he ran and disappeared back into the woods. Breathing heavily and sweating, he hid in the shadows zigzagging among the trees and down the two blocks back to his car. As he got in and slowly pulled away from the curb, he heard police sirens wailing in the distance. Alvin looked over at the briefcase resting on the passenger seat, wiped his brow, and maneuvered the backroads to the home he shared with his mother.

Somewhere between 12:30 and 1 a.m., Alvin's Nissan rolled up into his driveway and came to rest alongside the house almost touching the garage door. He waited for a moment after turning off the car before grabbing the briefcase off the seat and getting out. He didn't walk to the house, but instead, went to the side of the garage and entered it through the locked door. Alvin turned on the light in the windowless, custom-built structure he had worked on for several years and walked directly to the workbench he had designed and built himself. The back of the workbench consisted of a large pegboard covered in small tools. One end of the pegboard was attached to hidden hinges. He reached behind the other end and gently swung open the door-like pegboard revealing shallow shelves that contained several handguns and various stolen items. Alvin placed the briefcase onto one of the shelves, closed the peg board, and moved several items onto the workbench up against it. He turned off the light, locked the door, and entered the home where his mom was sound asleep.

# Chapter 59

Mike McShea had become fascinated at the potential opportunities of using Ryan after the success he had with Alberto Cerrone. He spent his nights researching past crimes such as bank robberies, armored car robberies, and drug deals that involved large, unaccounted amounts of cash. The Alvin Bradford case intrigued him, and it was one of several possibilities he wanted to pursue.

Several police cars had responded to the calls of shots fired shortly after midnight in the area of Liberty Park and found two dead bodies, one near a briefcase loaded with high grade cocaine, and the other slumped thirty feet away at the base of a tree. They suspected that a drug deal had been interrupted and, in their haste to get away, the drugs were left behind.

The police had little to go on, other than a few spent shell casings from a small caliber .22 handgun. Investigators canvassed the area and were encouraged when several homeowners located behind the park and along neighboring streets revealed to police that their homes were equipped with security cameras that might be of help.

Two homes located behind the park provided a grainy recording of a thin, darkly clothed figure walking away from the wooded area carrying something in his hand. Several other homeowners a block away also provided recordings of a suspicious person walking in the shadows past their home. Investigators continued talking to other homeowners along this route and were eventually able to piece together enough video footage to observe Alvin Bradford entering his parked Nissan Sentra.

The police then had a description of the vehicle to work with and a timeframe that the car was on the road. They coordinated with the city's transportation department to access their traffic surveillance recordings, which normally were used for monitoring high volume and problematic intersections. It didn't take long for investigators to identify Alvin's vehicle cruising through one of the monitored intersections at thirty minutes past midnight.

Less than a week after the killings in Liberty Park, Alvin was identified as the owner of the Nissan and brought in for questioning. A search of his mother's home turned up the .22 caliber gun used to kill Vic Santoro as police grilled Alvin for hours, presenting him with all their video and ballistic evidence. He eventually admitted to being out that night but had no intention of killing anyone and was only defending himself when he stumbled upon the drug deal.

He explained that he hid behind a tree and witnessed the first man getting shot, then the killer pointed his gun and walked toward the tree. Alvin confessed that, as Vic Santoro was about to find him, he pulled out his own gun and shot in self-defense.

At his trial, the jury found Alvin Bradford guilty of manslaughter and sentenced him to eight years in prison. With good time served, he hoped to get out earlier than that and return to his mother's house where, unbeknownst to anyone else, a briefcase full of cash would be waiting for him. His plan would then be to pack his things, head west, and start a new life.

A large drug deal, a dead drug dealer, a briefcase full of high-grade cocaine left at the scene, and one remaining witness. McShea reasoned that it only made sense that if a large drug deal takes place, two things are usually present: drugs and cash. There was never any mention of cash being recovered at the scene. He thought that perhaps Ryan could provide some insight.

# Chapter 60

Ryan and his son, Aaron, took turns dipping their sponges into the soapy bucket and wiping down the side of the Camry, while Jason stood by with the hose ready to rinse. "Okay, we're done on this side, rinse her down!" Ryan barked. Jason aimed and pointed the spray at the car's side but wound up soaking his dad instead. Ryan didn't seem to mind receiving some welcome relief from the hot sun.

Lisa poked her head out the side door, careful to stay out of reach of Jason's aim. "Ryan, phone call," then she ducked back into the house.

"Guys, keep going, I'll be back in a few minutes." Ryan grabbed a towel and dried his hands and arms. He walked by Lisa, giving her a look as if to ask who was on the phone, but got nothing more than a shrug of the shoulders. "I'll get it in the office."

"Hello?" he said slightly out of breath.

"Ryan, this is Mike McShea, sorry to bother you on a Saturday. It's important, do you have time to meet with me sometime today or tomorrow? Whichever is more convenient for you."

Ryan's tone turned cool. *Could this be about the killing of Alberto Cerrone*, Ryan thought. "I can make it later this afternoon, say, three o'clock?"

"Great. I'll be at the far end of the parking lot in Pullen Park. See you then." Ryan heard McShea hang up and stared at the phone in his hand. He looked up and saw Lisa in the doorway with a dish towel in her hand. He wasn't sure just how long she was standing there but he assumed she heard him say he'd be somewhere at three o'clock.

"That was Agent McShea," Ryan said flatly.

"Isn't he the one you helped with that Gastonia bank robbery a while back?"

"Yeah. Not sure what he wants this time, but he says it's important. He glanced at his watch and still had over two hours before the meeting. "I better get back out there and make sure those two aren't cleaning the inside of my car with that hose!" Lisa leaned against the door as Ryan sprinted past her to rejoin the boys, not noticing her concerned look.

# Chapter 61

Ryan stripped off his soggy clothes and jumped in the shower. He had thirty minutes to shower, get dressed, and make the twenty-minute drive to Pullen Park. *Screw him,* he thought. *Why should I jump every time he makes a request?* He hadn't heard from Mike McShea in nearly two months and the sudden urgency of another meeting today was putting him in a foul mood. After drying off, he wrapped the towel around his waist and walked into the bedroom.

"Are you okay? Seems this guy always gets under your skin." Lisa asked, knowing that he wasn't.

Ryan's exhaled heavily. "Yeah, I'm fine. There's just something about this McShea guy that rubs me the wrong way. We can talk about it when I get back." He sat on the edge of the bed, ran his hands through his wet hair, and glanced over at the clock on his nightstand. The digital numbers flipped to 2:38 p.m.

Lisa turned to leave the room but stopped when she got to the door and spun around. "Do me one favor?" she asked looking him straight in the eye. "Keep me in the loop this time?"

"How about you guys do mom's car now? I've got to run an errand, so I'll see you in a little while." Ryan backed the Camry slowly down the driveway, turned, and cautiously weaved around parked cars as he made his way out of the sub-division. A beautiful sun-drenched afternoon was not going to be ruined rushing to meet someone else's agenda. Today, he purposely drove in the slower right-hand lane, enjoyed the breeze circulating throughout the car, and smirked at the vehicles that blew past him in their anxious pursuit to wherever it was they had to be.

Mike McShea's car found the lone blanket of shade at the far end of the parking lot. He turned off his engine, lowered his windows, and watched a large group of cyclists in brightly colored tops gather a short distance away, checking their bikes and sucking down bottles of water. His eyes, however, never lost sight of the park's entrance. At ten minutes past three o'clock, his fingers began nervously tapping on the steering wheel as a second group of cyclists entered the park followed by a silver Camry. He sat stoically as Ryan pulled up alongside his car.

Both men exited their vehicles; McShea dressed in khakis and long sleeve shirt as if attending a business meeting, and Ryan in his dark blue Dockers shorts and a polo. Neither looked like they were there to enjoy a day at the park as they ambled over to a familiar bench.

"Thanks for seeing me on such short notice," McShea said almost apologetically. "Ryan, you have an extraordinary gift," and his voice tailed off. He looked off into the distance, speaking as if no one was there next to him. "I can't imagine being able to witness something that no one else has seen, or at least reported to have seen."

Ryan was quick to respond. "A gift? Sometimes I really wonder about that! And who's to say that gifts can't be taken away as abruptly as they're received?" Ryan hoped he had gotten his point across. "Okay, I'm listening."

"This one's a bit complicated. There's a drug deal and a double homicide. But it's also personal." McShea thought about this approach for almost a week. There had to appear to be more to it than *looking for lost cash.* "An arrest was made, and the fellow is now in prison. He was living at the time with his mother, who happens to be a friend of a close friend." McShea then continued with his lie. "She said she had no knowledge of her son's crime, but there are some who don't believe her story."

Ryan sat there picking at his fingernails and turned to look at McShea. "A drug deal, double homicide, a guy in prison, and a mom who knows nothing about it. Got it. So, what exactly are you asking me to do?"

"Two things. First, see what *really* happened at the so-called drug deal, and second, see what happened when the son, Alvin Bradford, returned to his mother's home that night. All the details are in an envelope I have for you in my car."

They stood up and McShea had one more thing to say. "Ryan, as much as I'd want your assistance on all the cases that come across my desk, I know it's unrealistic, and something you're probably not too keen about. I'll respect your privacy after this. But of course, if you ever *do* want to volunteer your services, feel free to contact me any time, day or night."

Ryan gave a nod and they returned to their vehicles. McShea opened the passenger door and grabbed the large envelope resting on the seat. "Let me know if you have any questions."

"I'll give you a call when," Ryan said as he settled in behind the steering wheel. He looked over at the envelope, put the car in gear, and slowly drove away. Just before turning to exit the park, his eyes glanced up at the rear-view mirror. Mike McShea's car hadn't moved yet. He mumbled to no one in the car, "So, you're going to respect my privacy, huh?" Ryan wasn't quite sure he believed it. He called Lisa's cell phone. "Hey Lis, I'm on my way home."

"Well, how did it go?" she asked cautiously.

"Usual stuff. A couple of unknowns; he'd like some insight. I'll be home in about fifteen minutes. We can talk about it then." Ryan hung up a little angry with himself at how vague he had just been.

Lisa placed her cell phone down and resumed assembling the ingredients to prepare dinner. While waiting for the pot of water on the stove to boil, she made one quick entry in her journal, then hurriedly scooped up a few loose papers from the kitchen table, tossed everything into a binder, and secured them away in her closet.

# Chapter 62

The sound of forks scraping plates replaced the usual table banter that was often typical at dinnertime. The boys usually took their cue from their parents but tonight, neither had much to say. Ryan powered down his plate of lasagna, placed his utensils onto the plate, and sat back fondling his wine glass. He and Lisa exchanged silent glances across from each other.

Then Jason spoke up. "Mom, we're done. Can we have a piece of that chocolate cake?"

Seeing that their plates were empty, she nodded. "Sure, but put your plates in the sink first. If you promise not to make a mess, you can eat upstairs."

Hearing this, the boys raced to the sink with their dishes, grabbed new plates, and each cut a generous slice of cake Lisa had made earlier in the day. A few moments later, the sound of footsteps up the stairs gave way to the sound of a shutting door. Lisa pushed aside her half-eaten plate, reached for her wine glass, and gave Ryan a long, silent stare.

He placed his glass back on the table and sat up straight, knowing full well she was waiting for him to speak. "There was a drug deal in the Charlotte area almost a year ago. Two men were killed, and they have a suspect in one of the killings."

"So, he wants to know who killed the other person?" Lisa asked as if cross-examining him. On the drive back from his meeting with McShea, Ryan promised himself he would be as open as possible with her. "Not exactly. They have someone in custody who admitted to killing one of them in self-defense. This person that he killed *apparently* killed the other one."

"Okay, so both killings have been solved and one guy is in jail. What's left to solve?" Ryan didn't anticipate the probing questions.

"According to the police report, a large amount of drugs were found at the scene." Ryan got up and retrieved McShea's envelope from his office. "Here, this is what McShea gave me. What you won't see in there is the real reason, I think, that McShea wants help with this. The mother of the man being held is a friend of a friend of McShea's, and he thinks she might somehow be involved."

"The mother is a friend of a friend? Really?" Lisa said dripping with sarcasm. She pulled the papers out of the envelope and laid them out in front of her. Her eyes slowly read through the first page. "So, this guy just so happened to be out walking late one night, was carrying a gun, and hid behind a tree to watch a drug deal go down?" Lisa's tone implied that a point was about to be made. "Both guys in the drug deal are dead, and the only survivor is someone who happened to stumble upon this on a leisurely night walk through the park?"

Ryan certainly didn't expect the cynicism and barrage of questions she was aiming at him. "Lisa, this guy was a criminal as well. He was carrying a gun, no doubt looking for his own opportunity that night. Anyway, they got the guy."

Lisa looked up from the page she was studying. "Look, I'm no detective, but when there's a drug deal, isn't there usually an exchange of drugs for money?"

Ryan's was slow to speak. "I'm sure it's there somewhere. Either way, if I can get back there, I'll keep an eye out for it." His nonchalant response was an attempt to hide this suspicion he hadn't thought about when he read what McShea had given him. His distrust for McShea rose to a new level. "On a positive note, McShea did promise me when we left each other today that from here on, he's going to respect my privacy. I took that as *no more calls*." He reached across the table and grabbed the two pages and inserted them back into the envelope.

"Can I refill your glass?" she asked.

"No thanks. I need to sit down and think through the details in here," he said pointing to the envelope. Ryan stood up, walked around the table, and kissed Lisa on the forehead. "I'm *really* hoping this is the end of it." Clutching the envelope, he walked down the hallway to his man cave.

Lisa opened the kitchen junk draw and pulled out a small notepad and pen. *Charlotte – Liberty Park – drug deal – two dead – suspect caught*. She folded the piece of paper and stuffed it into her back pocket.

# Chapter 63

Ryan had read through the details of the Liberty Park crime, noting the date, time, and the park's location. McShea had asked him to report on what really happened at the park that night and determine whether or not the mother was, in any way, involved. Ryan made a habit of preparing notes about the details of wherever it was he was being asked to "visit." This latest request from McShea put more questions in Ryan's head. He looked down at the notes on his index card.

*Is the mother involved? – Was she at the crime scene? – Did she lie to police? – Was she aware of her son's activities?*

Meanwhile, Lisa had her own suspicions that she kept to herself: – *Was there any money exchanged at the drug deal? – Was Alvin Bradford a part of this drug deal or did he just happen to stumble upon it? – What is McShea's connection to this "friend of a friend?"*

The details in that envelope given to him by McShea provided the exact date and approximate time of around midnight. Inserting himself there an hour or so before all the action takes place should provide the insight needed into who was involved and how the sequence of events unfolded. He rehashed the details in his head for almost two hours until his eyelids became heavy.

When he emerged from his office, most of the lights had already been turned out and the house was quiet. Ryan quietly pushed open the bedroom door and saw Lisa propped up in bed reading. As soon as he entered, she closed her book and turned off the light on her nightstand leaving the room dimly lit by the light on his side of the bed.

"Good night. See you in the morning," was all she said, turning on her side and pulling the covers up to her neck.

"Good night, Lis," he whispered. A few moments later, Ryan crawled into bed, reached over, and turned out the light. The moment his head hit the pillow; his focus was on Liberty Park.

At some point during the night, Ryan's cerebral journey landed him at the edge of Liberty Park in Charlotte on a walking trail that was described in detail in the file.

*The air was thick, and it was an eerily dark and windless night. From where he stood, Ryan could make out a bench up ahead with a line of trees as a backdrop. According to Alvin Bradford, he hid behind those trees and watched a drug deal that led to a murder. Ryan walked to the trees, turned, and looked back at the bench to confirm that what Alvin testified to, was consistent to what he was seeing now.*

*Ryan leaned against a tree, his eyes scanning the area on both sides of the old wooden bench until they were alerted to movement. Emerging from the tree line around fifty feet from where he stood, Ryan could see a shadowy figure walking cautiously toward the bench. Perhaps another fifty feet further down, a second figure came out of the woods. Both carried what looked like a briefcase. The two met near the bench and began to speak in a hushed tone, nervously turning their heads, perhaps wary that others might be nearby.*

*Ryan continued to watch the two figures by the bench discuss their business, occasionally gesturing down to the briefcases they held close to their side. A movement of an approaching figure from the shadows of the woods got Ryan's attention. He assumed this to be Alvin Bradford and watched as Alvin crept slowly to a nearby tree, shielded from what was going on near the bench. Alvin hid behind the tree as if curious and afraid, as opposed to being a criminal accomplice to a drug deal. Ryan's eyes shifted back to the two men as one of them placed his briefcase on the bench, opening it for the other to observe its contents. After a brief look, he appeared satisfied and, with a nod of the head, the briefcase was closed.*

*A distinct snapping sound shattered the silence. Ryan observed a wide-eyed Alvin squat down holding his breath in fear and peering around the tree at the two men. A sudden movement by one of them was followed by the sound of a gunshot. One figure fell to the ground while the other, still clutching his briefcase, turned and began walking toward the source of the sound with his gun extended in front of him and his head swiveling from side to side. Ryan stood several feet from Alvin and watched him pull out a small handgun from his waistband. He held it next to his head pointing toward the sky as the man got closer. In a sudden move, Alvin sprang to his feet and fired two shots at the approaching figure. With the gun in one hand and the briefcase now loosely clutched by the other, the man slumped at the base of the tree and remained motionless.*

*Alvin's eyes were wide, and he was panting, as he looked down at the briefcase. Ryan stood next to Alvin and watched him bend down and open the case, letting out a gasp at the sight of the neatly stacked rows of cash. Quickly shutting it, he stood up, took a hasty look at the other motionless figure by the bench, then sprinted back through the woods. Ryan lost sight of him but was sure he was heading for his car and back to his mother's home.*

Ryan's gaze into the dark woods slowly began to fade, replaced by the room's morning light. He rolled onto his back, pulled the sheets up to his chin, and stared at the ceiling. Lisa had just returned to bed from a trip to the bathroom, and he turned his head on the pillow to face her.

"Good morning," she whispered, before recognizing that faraway look in his eyes.

A moment passed before Ryan could find words. "Wow, some night," he said. "It was pretty much the way it was reported. Except..."

"Except what?" Lisa asked as she laid back down next to him.

"You were right," he told her. "Two dead bodies, a briefcase of drugs, and a briefcase of cash. I actually only saw the briefcase filled with cash. The other briefcase was by the first guy who got shot and I assume it had the drugs. And wouldn't you know that guy who supposedly stumbled upon a drug deal was the one who walked away with the cash!"

Lisa ran her fingers through his hair, watching him trying to process the dream he had just woken from.

"Lis, do you think this Alvin guy knew all along that a drug deal was going to take place? Maybe the plan was for him to kill them both and take off with the loot. I don't know. He looked awfully scared and not really the tough guy type at all."

"So where does the mother fit in with all of this?" Lisa innocently asked.

"I have no clue. I didn't see her there. Maybe she drove him and was waiting in the getaway car. That will be my next visit – hopefully tonight."

# Chapter 64

Ryan reached over and grabbed his iPhone off the nightstand to let his boss know that he wasn't coming in to work. He needed time to think about last night and walk through everything that's happened since Sgt. Joe Ramos handed him over to Mike McShea. Ryan threw on a pair of shorts and a creased T-shirt and walked barefoot to the kitchen.

"Casual dress day at work today?" Lisa asked with a grin.

"I'm taking the day off. No meetings today, no deadlines to meet – I think I deserve a day off," he said in a light-hearted boast.

Lisa knew exactly why Ryan had taken the day off. "A lot to think about from last night, huh?"

"Yeah, that too. I'm also going to tell McShea that I'm having issues with my dreams, and he may not be able to depend on me anymore. You know, I've had reservations about this guy from day one. And these cases he's asked me to help with...?" Ryan's voice trailed off as he wandered around the kitchen with an empty coffee cup. "Any plans today?"

"The girls are getting together at Janet's house down the block to exchange recipes; then it's off to the mall. You've got the whole place to yourself for a while." Lisa disappeared into the bedroom as Ryan grabbed a banana off the counter, then walked to his office. He stood by his desk rehearsing the call he was about to make to McShea.

After the kids had left for school and Lisa was out the door, he punched in the numbers for Mike McShea, who answered on the first ring as if expecting the call. "Ryan?"

"Hello Mike. Can you meet me at the Waffle House on Highway 64 at ten o'clock?"

"Sure, were you–"

"Great, see you then," Ryan said, and he hung up. The details from his visit to Liberty Park the previous night were still fresh in his mind and Ryan was eager to provide this information and move on to the second part of McShea's request; the mother's possible involvement. Ryan also planned on using this morning's meeting to inform McShea that he was having some physical issues and that the dreams may not be reliable much longer. He hoped that McShea would buy it and finally leave him alone.

McShea glared at his cell phone, not at all pleased with, or accustomed to, being given instructions like that. He pulled out a leather binder from his desk drawer and flipped the pages until he reached a blank one to record a few notes about his discussion and plans for the day. He was anxious to hear what Ryan had to say today.

Ryan was already parked near the Waffle House entrance when McShea's car turned into the lot. Already seated in a booth by the window, he locked eyes with McShea as he slowly cruised by and parked next to Ryan's Camry. When they met inside, the smiles each had masked the suspicion they were beginning to have for each other. McShea joined Ryan in the booth and ordered a coffee.

"You seemed eager to meet this morning," McShea said.

"A lot going on with work and at home. But I don't think that's what you want to hear. I paid a visit last night to Liberty Park and saw your friend Alvin." Ryan had decided before the meeting that he would control the conversation.

Ryan stopped talking when the server brought McShea's coffee to the table. He took a sip and waited for Ryan to continue.

"It all pretty much happened the way Alvin described it. I did see the two individuals in the park discussing the drug deal. While that was going on, Alvin appeared to approach the area and hide behind a tree to observe. When he moved slightly, he made a sudden noise and it looked like one of the figures panicked and shot the other one. He then walked toward Alvin with his gun drawn and just as he got to a tree next to where Alvin was hiding, Alvin pulled out a gun, jumped out and shot him."

McShea nodded, not seeming too surprised by anything that was said. The investigation concluded that Alvin's gun was only used to kill Vic Santoro who was approaching him. It was Vic Santoro's gun that had killed the apparent drug dealer by the bench.

"So, what happened then?" McShea asked as if interrogating Ryan.

"Well, Alvin stood there a moment, then he bent down and opened up the briefcase that was dropped by the guy he just shot. I got a good look – it was filled to the brim with cash. Anyway, he shuts the case and takes off back into the woods. I was about to follow but... my time was up!"

"So, you don't think he was involved in this drug deal in any way?" McShea asked, in an attempt to steer away from any thoughts about Alvin leaving with the cash.

"From what I saw, no. He looked scared shitless from the moment he was hiding behind that tree right until he ran out of there," Ryan said with confidence.

*A briefcase filled to the brim with cash*. McShea had just been given confirmation of something he had hoped for. Drugs were found at the scene, but nothing was ever mentioned about cash being recovered. Now he knew why. "Okay, but just the same, I'd still like to confirm that his mother was not at all involved. That should tie this one up for me." McShea had to make Ryan think there was a mother angle to all of this.

Ryan knew exactly what McShea wanted him to do – make a visit to the house when Alvin got home and see what happens. The two of them spent the next fifteen minutes discussing random local events until their cups were empty. That seemed to signal it was time to get up and leave.

As Ryan opened his car door to get in, he turned to McShea. "I'll give you a call when I've got something," once again being the one to call the shots. Just before he pulled out of the parking lot, he glanced up at his rear-view mirror and watched McShea still seated in his car. *Something isn't quite right about that guy*, he thought.

# Chapter 65

On the drive home, Ryan dissected the conversation with McShea, searching for anything to confirm the uneasy feeling he had. He suddenly remembered what Lisa had said about the report he shared with her; *there was no mention of money being recovered at the scene.* Ryan realized that when he had mentioned the briefcase of money and that Alvin took off with it, McShea ever so slightly sat up straighter in his chair but said nothing about it. *The guy makes off with a briefcase full of loot, it's not found anywhere in the police report, and McShea acts disinterested*? Ryan pushed down harder on the accelerator. Too many thoughts were flooding his mind and he wanted to get home quickly before he lost any of them.

He rushed through the side door into the kitchen. "Lisa?" Silence. He kept walking straight to his office, leaving the door ajar so he could listen for Lisa or the kids. Ryan sat down, reached into the drawer, and pulled out several folders which contained all the cases he had assisted on, for both Ramos and McShea. The question that still burned inside of him was, *why did Sgt. Ramos so abruptly hand him over to FBI agent McShea and then simply disappear*? He recalled that day at the park and how helpless and meek Sgt. Ramos had appeared, as if embarrassed by the introduction and sudden exit he had to make. Oddly, McShea has never mentioned Ramos's name since that day. Ryan couldn't dwell on that right now. He turned his attention to the folders in front of him.

The first one he opened contained notes and descriptions of the cases Ryan assisted with. Initially, it was Ryan who called in the unsolicited anonymous tip. Lisa had suggested a few of the unsolved cases and a few others resulted from dreams Ryan had that he confirmed in local news articles shortly thereafter. There was only one case that stood out where Sgt. Ramos reached out for help from Ryan: the abduction and unsolved murder of young Kevin Conlin. He read through all his notes and news articles associated with that case and nowhere did the name Mike McShea or any reference to the FBI show up.

Ryan reached for the folder labeled *McShea*. In it were his personal notes and the descriptions provided by McShea for the three requests made over the past four or five months – the bank robbery in Gastonia, Alberto Cerrone, and Alvin Bradford. The Gastonia request was for nothing more than a description of a getaway vehicle. McShea's description of the case noted that it was a late morning robbery in downtown Gastonia and the two robbers fled the bank and disappeared into an alley way. Ryan was able to visit the bank on the day of the robbery and observe the robbers getting into their vehicle. He remembered providing the car's description and license plate to McShea and never heard another word about the case.

Ryan moved the wireless mouse across the screen and clicked on the internet icon. In the search bar he typed *Gastonia bank robbery, April 14*. Several articles from different news outlets appeared, and they all seemed to contain the same information. After browsing three of the articles, one detail in all of them jumped out and caught his attention – the suspects had not been caught but the car, believed to be the getaway car, had been found abandoned later that day in the next town over. *The car was found abandoned.*

Ryan had to read that again to make sure. He then looked down at his own scribbled notes of the discussion he had with McShea, which indicated that the agent asked him to get a description of the getaway car. The date of that discussion with McShea took place on June 8. Ryan leaned back in his chair and slowly shook his head. "What the...?" he said out loud to no one in the room. After a moment of sitting paralyzed in his chair, he sprang up and started working the keyboard. The next entry into the search bar was *Alberto Cerrone.*

About a dozen articles popped up relating to Alberto Cerrone and his unsolved murder. Ryan carefully read each one, noting how they described Cerrone, his lifestyle in Raleigh, suspicions of his involvement in the drug industry, and his apparent gang-related murder. Several articles also mentioned that the police performed a search of his home which revealed a safe containing large amounts of drugs and stolen jewelry. Ryan stopped to reflect on that night he had visited Cerrone's home and observed the contents of the safe. He remembered it being loaded with cash, however, not one of the articles mentioned anything about cash being found along with the drugs and jewelry. Ryan ran his hand across his forehead. He had seen the cash in the safe and reported everything he had witnessed to Mike McShea the next day. A week later, Alberto Cerrone is found murdered in an apparent drug-related killing along the side of the road not far from his home. Ryan grabbed a pen and wrote down the location of where they found Cerrone dead in his car.

Ryan then positioned the cursor on the search bar and typed in *Liberty Park – Alvin Bradford.* Several Raleigh-area news articles popped up on the screen and he opened and reviewed them, one by one. Ryan is familiar with all the details that the police reports provided to the news outlets; two men murdered in a drug deal in Liberty Park and a third man arrested and charged with manslaughter of one of the victims. It also stated that drugs were recovered from the scene. Ryan paused and reread that last sentence again. There was no mention of cash at the scene or recovered during the arrest of Alvin Bradford, even though Ryan witnessed him walking off with the briefcase full of cash. There was one more visit Ryan needed to make.

# Chapter 66

"So, did you enjoy a little peace and quiet today?" Lisa asked after entering the house. Ryan had heard the car pull up the driveway and was already in the kitchen waiting for her when she walked in.

"Yeah, it was a pretty quiet day. Did you come home with any interesting recipes from your get-together at Janet's? Always in the mood for something new!"

Ryan wasn't saying anything about his day and Lisa knew better than to press the issue. *He'll talk when he's ready*, she thought. "A couple of fun desserts the kids might like. Other than that, nothing that appealed to me," Lisa said before heading down the hallway. Ryan sensed that his "quiet day" response would be interpreted by Lisa as him not wanting to talk.

"Hey Lis, how 'bout I make dinner tonight?" he yelled down the hallway. "I've got this great recipe where I throw some hot dogs on the grill and encapsulate them in specially toasted buns! You know the kids are crazy about that!"

A voice from the bedroom was quick to reply. "That sounds great! While you're preparing your specialty, I'll try out one of my new desserts! By the way, did you talk to your FBI friend today?" Ryan stopped in his tracks and rolled his eyes. He was hoping to avoid the discussion, but Lisa knew when she left this morning that he'd planned to meet with McShea. She didn't want to wait until the kids got home to have this discussion.

"Oh yeah, we met. I filled him in on everything I observed last night, and it fell right in line with what he expected." Ryan didn't wait for a response and slipped out the back door to clean the grill.

The dinner atmosphere that night felt like the old days before Ryan experienced his change. Jason and Aaron were thrilled to eat dad's specialty dinner, mom's new dessert was a big hit, and the kitchen was filled with laughter and goofy stories. Outside, the sun disappeared, the boys journeyed upstairs, and Ryan and Lisa kicked back together on the couch.

"How about we skip the news tonight, okay?" Lisa asked.

"Fine with me. How about we stare at the weather channel for a while?" he said trying to act serious.

"Perfect," she said, turning off the TV, tossing the remote across the room, and cuddling in his arms. They remained like that in silence for the next hour.

Ryan's head tilted back and rested on the back of the couch, and his eyes closed as thoughts began to drift toward Alvin Bradford and the "visit" he wanted to make that night. He couldn't stop thinking about the mother's possible involvement and the briefcase. And then Lisa broke the silence.

"This was really nice, here with you now and our dinner with the kids. It was a nice night." The message she was sending was loud and clear.

"Yeah, I know. We'll have more of this. I promise." The sincerity in his voice was genuine. He kissed her and they both got up off the couch. Lisa headed for the stairway to check on the boys while Ryan grabbed a coke from the fridge and disappeared into his office.

After saying good night to the boys, Lisa descended the stairs and went straight to the bedroom. On the way she paused in front of the closed office door, shook her head slowly, and continued to her room. When Ryan entered a short while later, the light on her nightstand was already out and she was asleep. His feet shuffled silently across the carpet until he reached the bed. He carefully pulled back the sheets, slipped into bed, and rolled onto his side. For the last hour, he had thought of nothing except Alvin Bradford's mother's house and the timeframe he needed to be there. He closed his eyes, pressed his cheek into the pillow, and drifted off.

*Ryan was standing in front of the house late on the night of the Liberty Park drug deal and murder. The street was dark, and the old, one-story dwellings packed close together didn't hint at opulence among the residents living there. A lit porch light was the only light on at Alvin's mother's home and it provided a soft glow on the tall grass in the front yard. Ryan didn't have long to wait until he saw the headlights approaching fast from several blocks away. He stood motionless as Alvin's Nissan turned into the driveway and pulled up to the garage. Alvin quickly turned the car off but remained seated. Ryan walked up the driveway to get a closer look just as Alvin emerged from his car, briefcase in hand. He walked up to the side of the garage and entered it through a side door as Ryan followed close behind. The first thing Ryan noticed was how organized and well-constructed the interior of the garage appeared, a stark contrast to the home it belonged to. Precision-cut shelves contained power tools and a solidly built workbench with a pegboard background was neatly stocked with every tool a woodworker would need. Ryan watched as Alvin approached the workbench and reached in at one end of the pegboard, opening it up as if turning a page in a book. When the entire board swiveled open, it revealed shallow hidden shelves harboring assorted jewelry and other apparent stolen property. Alvin placed the briefcase on one of the shelves and closed the pegboard back to its original position. Very clever, Ryan thought. Ryan followed Alvin out of the garage, as he walked toward the house and silently entered the dark kitchen. His mother was apparently sound asleep in her room. Alvin retreated to his bedroom while Ryan sat down in the dark at the kitchen table. He didn't remember anything else until he was awakened by Lisa closing the bathroom door.*

Ryan's eyes cracked open, and he thought about what he'd just seen at the mother's house. Alvin's workshop was well-equipped with all the finest tools of a professional woodworker, and the pegboard that secretly opened to reveal hidden shelves was not some standard feature found in a typical garage. He was convinced Alvin had constructed it to accommodate his trade as a thief, and as far as he could tell, the mother probably didn't have a clue about any of it.

# Chapter 67

Months had passed since the meeting in Pullen Park with McShea and Ryan, and Sergeant Joe Ramos had settled back into his routine of policing the small, tight-knit community of Fulton. There were times when he certainly could have used Ryan Field's assistance, however, Agent Mike McShea made it quite clear to disengage. Ramos, though, still wasn't comfortable having an FBI agent nearby in Raleigh who possessed the full intel of his background. He considered a few options to relocate and disappear but realized laying low and doing his job in Fulton was probably his best option. His thoughts were abruptly interrupted when Sarah poked her head through the doorway.

"You've got a call from a Mr. Jared Henderson on line 2. Are you in?" she asked. Ramos furrowed his brow and stared at her for a moment as if trying to place the name.

"Joe?" she asked a little louder.

"Did he say what's it's about?" Ramos asked looking up at her.

"Nope. Just asked for you specifically," Sarah replied, impatiently waiting for an answer.

"Yeah, sure, I'll take it." Ramos assumed it was just someone following up on a specific case and was looking for status. "This is Sgt. Ramos." His tone was cool and abrupt.

"Sgt. Ramos, this is FBI Agent Jared Henderson, thank you for taking my call. I'd like–"

Before he could continue, Ramos cut him off. "Agent Henderson, if you're calling in regard to Ryan Field, we no longer communicate, and I'm happy to keep it that way."

*Ryan Field*? Jared had overheard McShea mention that name in his meeting with Ramos during their meeting in McShea's office. He wondered now if this Ryan Field could be the third person at that meeting in Pullen Park. "Yes sir, I understand but I'm not calling about Ryan Field. I would like to talk with you and was hoping we could meet - perhaps tonight?" he asked in a polite and respectful tone.

Ramos was caught off guard and didn't immediately respond. He wasn't exactly endeared to the FBI, Mike McShea in particular, however his interest was piqued by agent Henderson's request, especially since it didn't have anything to do with Ryan Field. "Sure, do you know where the Crabtree Ale House is on the north side of Raleigh?"

"I can find it," Jared replied. "And when I see you, I'll flag you down."

"Okay, I'll be there at eight o'clock." Ramos hung up and walked over to close the door. *Flag me down? He knows who I am?* He leaned up against the side of the window and stared out at a quiet street, the occasional car passing by, and the deliberate gait of the locals shuffling along the sidewalks. He didn't know who Jared Henderson was other than a local FBI agent. Most likely he had ties to Mike McShea. But, since this was supposedly *not* about Ryan Field, Ramos could only believe it had to do with his own past and another FBI agent wanting to use it against him for "a favor."

# Chapter 68

Ryan pulled to the side of the road two blocks from his home and punched in the number for Mike McShea. Once it started ringing on the other end, he resumed his drive to work and waited for McShea to answer.

"Mike, good morning, this is Ryan."

"Good morning, Ryan. Everything ok?"

"Hope I didn't catch you at a bad time. I'm on my way to work right now and may have some information for you."

"That's great. Just let me know when you're available."

Ryan was amused at how laid back and relaxed McShea tried to sound.

"I'll give you a call sometime tonight when I get off work," Ryan said in an even more casual manner.

Toward the end of the workday, Ryan became less productive, as he sat staring at the picture of Lisa and the boys that served as the screensaver on his twenty-inch monitor. His thoughts drifted back to the previous night and Alvin Bradford.

He picked up his cell phone that was resting on a notepad and punched in McShea's number. "I'm on my way to the park now," was all Ryan said.

"See you there," McShea replied.

Pullen Park was a twenty-minute drive; plenty of time to rehash last night's events in his head and to let McShea know that from here on, *he* would be the one to decide whether to assist in any more cases. He felt his grip tightening on the steering wheel as he turned into the park's entrance and carefully passed a few bike riders. The parking lot was half-filled, and he slowly drove down the aisle until McShea's black Ford came into view parked near the end of the lot.

McShea got out and walked leisurely in the direction of a

familiar bench they'd met at long before. Ryan caught up to him before he had time to sit.

"Why don't we take a walk instead?" Ryan offered. The path that wound through the park was long and wide, and much of it wound through a tree-covered maze eventually circling back to the parking lot.

McShea had learned to be wary whenever there was a deviation from a routine and his guard went up. "Sure, probably good to get in a little exercise. So, you said you had some information?"

Ryan maintained a slow, deliberate pace. "Interesting night for me. I was in Alvin's driveway when he got home around 1 a.m. The house was dark, but he didn't directly go in. Instead, he got out of his car with a briefcase and went directly into the garage." Ryan paused and waited for a response. McShea gave a casual nod, but Ryan sensed he was hanging on every word and anxious to hear more.

"You may have seen the house. It's old, a bit run down and, at least from the outside, doesn't look like it's been kept up. But the garage, now that's a different story."

"How so?" McShea finally uttered.

"A lot of custom features in there. Very nice woodwork, shelving, and a well-stocked workbench. It's clean and fairly organized, nothing like what you'd expect from what you see on the outside."

McShea's eyes widened ever so slightly. Inwardly, he was dying to know about the briefcase but didn't dare to ask.

"So, here's where it gets good. Alvin walks over to the workbench and reaches his hand behind one end of the pegboard that is full of small tools. Suddenly, the whole pegboard opens outward and hidden behind it are shelves containing some jewelry and other small items. His own personal hiding place! Well, he then placed the briefcase on one of the shelves and closed the pegboard to its original position. Nice custom feature, wouldn't you say?"

McShea's calm response was an attempt to hide his excitement at hearing the news. "Well, that makes some sense because Mr. Bradford told us that he had done some carpentry work in the past and had even done contracting work in a few new home developments in the past few years. Any thoughts about his mother perhaps being involved?"

"I don't think so. I was in the house afterward and there was no sign of her - must have been asleep. Anyway, my gut says she's not in the loop with this." Ryan stopped walking when they came to an opening that overlooked a small lake, picnic tables, and a playground. He surveyed the scene and exhaled deeply.

"Mike–"

Before he could say another word, McShea cut him off. "Ryan, you've been a great asset for us, and I know how stressful this all must be for you and your family. Unless it's a national emergency or of some critical importance, I just want you to know that I'm not going to put you through this anymore, unless of course you contact me and want to help with something. And of course, everything you and I have gone through will remain confidential." McShea extended an open hand. "It ends here."

"Thanks Mike, I appreciate that," Ryan said. "To be honest with you, I was really looking forward to getting back to a normal life with my family."

McShea nodded, and the two turned and made their way back to the parking lot, saying very little along the way. Ryan sat in his car as McShea gave one last smile and drove off.

*That was too easy,* Ryan thought. *The smiles, handshake, and that "thank you for all you've done" speech?* He still didn't care much for Mike McShea, but at least there was an understanding between them. All he wanted to do now was to just go home.

# Chapter 69

Agent Jared Henderson was seated at a high-top table against the wall facing the bar but having a clear view of the main entrance. Two coasters were on the table, one already supporting a tall draft beer. Dressed in jeans and a dark green polo shirt, Jared looked like any other sports bar patron there to watch a game on one of the many wide screen TVs. At 7:55, Jared noticed a small group gathered at the entrance, surveying the room for a table large enough to accommodate them. As they ventured in, Jared saw a lone figure behind them. He recognized Joe Ramos right away.

Joe Ramos had never met Jared Henderson before. Standing in the entranceway, he scanned the crowd for a lone male who looked like he might be expecting someone. There were several possibilities sitting at the bar, but Ramos knew that sitting at the bar was out of the question to conduct a private conversation. He slowly squeezed through the crowd to get a better look when his attention was caught by a hand raised into the air waving him over. He made his way through the crowded aisle to the table by the wall where Jared was sitting.

"Agent Henderson?"

Jared stood up and extended his hand. "Mr. Ramos, please call me Jared."

"Only if you call me Joe." After a brief pause, Ramos said, "You're not exactly what I expected."

"Because I'm African American?" Jared said with a grin.

Joe Ramos burst out laughing and sat down. "Uh no, I didn't expect you to be so young."

Ramos ordered a ginger ale from the server, and for the next fifteen minutes the two men exchanged small talk about living in Raleigh, family life, and their jobs.

Finally, Ramos, sat up, rested both elbows on the table and asked the obvious question. "Jared, what's on your mind? I know you must work with Mike McShea because you're aware of Ryan Field. And I think I've already told you that Mr. Field and I haven't spoken for several months."

"Joe, I never said I knew Ryan Field. Was he the third person in your meeting at Pullen Park with agent McShea?" Jared asked leaning forward.

"Yes he was, but I thought this meeting had nothing to do with him." Ramos wasn't quite sure where Jared was going with this, but he could easily see that he was fishing.

Jared took a long sip of beer, placed his glass on the coaster, and took a deep breath. Ramos was a skilled interrogator and recognized Jared's mannerisms as those exhibited by someone who was processing how to measure his words.

"Joe, I met Mike McShea when he stuck his head in my cubicle and requested some assistance with a background search for someone he was interested in. Never worked with him before, never even knew who he was."

"And that *someone* was me?" Ramos asked sternly. So, this is about me?

"That someone *is* you but you're not the reason I asked for this meeting. It has to do with McShea. You see, my assignment was to put together an in-depth background file on you, which I did, and then hand it over to McShea. And then – nothing. So, one day, I saw you in his office and overheard about a meeting you and him and some guy named Ryan Field were going to have in Pullen Park the next day at 1:30." Ramos held his hand over his mouth and listened intently trying to figure out where Jared was going with this.

"It's not at all that unusual to conduct private meetings so I didn't think much of it until McShea said he couldn't meet with me the next day at 1:30 because he had a *doctor's* appointment." Ramos nodded.

"McShea never followed up with me about what I had found in

your background, never heard another peep about you. In fact, he told me to keep everything confidential. He began working more behind a closed office door and didn't interact much with anyone. And then there was that Pullen Park meeting he had with you and Mr. Field that he wanted no one else to know about."

"Tell me something – how much do you know about Ryan Field?" Ramos quietly asked.

"Nothing. Only that there might be some link between the three of you. And knowing what I know about your history, I've been trying to figure out where Ryan Field fits in. But I want to say again, your history is *not* the reason for this meeting."

Ramos wanted to believe Jared but all he could think about now is that there's a second FBI agent aware of his past. Unlike his suspicion of McShea, Ramos felt comfortable in his conversation with Jared.

"Jared, I'm going to tell you something about Ryan Field that you may find incredible and hard to believe. I'm going to trust that you keep what we're talking about tonight, confidential."

Jared exhaled hard and looked straight into Ramos's eyes. "Joe, I was going to ask *you* to please not let McShea know that we met or had any discussion at all. I'll be honest with you; I don't trust him."

For the next hour, Joe Ramos described his interaction with Ryan Field and what he was capable of. He gave details of a few of the cases that were unsolved until Ryan was able to provide information that wasn't available before. Jared sat riveted throughout the discussion without saying a word. When the discussion turned to McShea and his involvement in all of this, Ramos's tone turned to anger.

"And then, one day I get a call from an FBI agent who's intrigued that I'm receiving all these anonymous tips and using them to solve crimes. The agent says he knows all about me and my past and basically backs me into a corner. So, what do I do? I offer up Ryan Field. I arrange the meeting in Pullen Park, McShea walks in, assumes control of Mr. Field, and basically tells me to take a walk." Ramos could see that Jared hung on every word and watched, as he tapped his fingers on the table preparing to respond.

"Joe, do you think you could contact Mr. Field and find out what McShea has been asking him to do? If Mr. Field is capable of doing what you say he can..." His voice trailed off.

# Chapter 70

Lisa heard Ryan's car roll up the driveway and come to a stop in front of the garage. He looked drained when he walked through the door. "How'd it go?" she asked in an upbeat tone.

"I told him everything about what I had seen at Alvin Bradford's home. When I mentioned about a hidden compartment in the garage where Alvin hid the briefcase of cash, he barely flinched. I told him that I didn't think the mother was involved and that was it. He thanked me, understood that I wanted to be left alone to get back to my family life, and that he would try not to contact me again. And of course, all of this is to remain confidential."

Ryan plopped down on a kitchen chair and Lisa walked over to rub his shoulders. "Do you trust him?" she asked.

"There's something not quite right about him," was all Ryan could say. "I had some doubts before, but now–"

"Just tell the son-of-a-bitch you're closed for business. Be done with him," Lisa fumed.

He looked up at her. "You're right, I'm done!"

Lisa had her own suspicions about McShea and would have had more had Ryan shared with her all the research he had done on the three cases McShea asked him to help with. Ryan didn't tell her that McShea asked him to identify a getaway car days after it had already been found. He also didn't tell her that police reports and news articles didn't report any missing cash in the Alberto Cerrone case. And now, Alvin Bradford was behind bars for eight years and there was a briefcase of cash from a drug deal hidden in his garage, and it appears that there are only two people, aside from Alvin Bradford, who know about its existence - himself and Mike McShea.

***

Later in the evening while watching the local news, Ryan's cell phone started buzzing on the kitchen counter. He didn't like answering calls during his quiet time at home, so he let it go to voice mail. Thirty seconds later, another call. This time Ryan jumped up and reached for the phone. The caller ID was *Mike McShea.*

"Mr. McShea, what can I do for you?" Ryan asked, as if talking to a telemarketer. Lisa heard Ryan mention McShea's name and instantly gave an angry eye roll in his direction.

"Ryan, I apologize for the late call. I know I said I wouldn't be bothering you anymore, but there are a few things I thought you should know, and I didn't want you to hear it from anyone else. I have some important information regarding Sergeant Joe Ramos that might be of interest to you." Ryan gave Lisa a quick glance and rolled his eyes as well before getting up and walking to his office, closing the door quietly behind him.

"Sgt. Ramos? I haven't spoken with him in months." Ryan sat down at his desk, grabbed a legal pad from the top drawer, and reached for a pen.

"I'm not saying you have – but he might be reaching out to *you* in the near future. You see, he's not who you think he is." McShea let that sink in for a moment.

Ryan sat in silence waiting for McShea to continue.

"He's got quite a history, and *Joe Ramos* isn't even his real name. It's Jose Ramos Alvarez. We've been investigating him for over a year. We know that he's been a friend to you and your wife, but we weren't quite sure what he was up to. All he told us was that you had provided a tip on a case he was working, but he wouldn't provide any details other than you had some unique ability. Regardless, I thought it was best to intervene that day in Pullen Park to say that I was going to work with you." McShea then looked down at his notes and a few drawings that described the timeline and interactions in the past six months between Ryan, Joe Ramos, and himself just to make sure his story made sense.

"So, what do I do if he contacts me?" Ryan asked.

"Be casual and if he requests to meet with you, find an excuse not to meet with him alone, and contact me right away." McShea scribbled notes as he spoke. "I'd appreciate it if you kept all of this to yourself until we make a formal case against him. Perhaps it would be better if your wife didn't know anything about this as well." Ryan didn't quite understand that last request, but there was too much to think about right now, so he didn't challenge it.

"There's more to this but I don't want to say any more over the phone. I know I promised we'd be through, but if we can get this last piece of information against Ramos, we'll have our case. Can you meet tomorrow night? I'll answer all your questions at that time."

"Can I ask you a question first? This guy has been a well-liked cop in Fulton for a long time. Why is he suddenly, a danger to our community?" Ryan couldn't grasp that Ramos was the villain that McShea was portraying him to be.

"It's complicated, but after we talk tomorrow, you'll understand everything," McShea said in a calm and reassuring tone.

"Isn't the park closed after dark?" Ryan asked.

"It is. But roughly half a mile past the park entrance there's the old Balco warehouse. There's a parking lot behind it around to the right. I can be there at nine o'clock – hope that's not too late."

"Nah, I've made late night runs to Walmart in the past, so this won't seem out of the ordinary," Ryan quickly replied. "See you then." Ryan hung up and remained at his desk thinking back to all the discussions and interactions he had with Joe Ramos and whether any red flags stood out. After a few minutes, he got up, walked to the door and flipped off the light. He expected Lisa to be waiting outside the office door, ready to grill him on his call with McShea. He hated to lie to her so instead, planned to downplay the call as McShea just wanting to thank him once again for all he's done. Ryan convinced himself that once the FBI goes public against

Joe Ramos, he could then reveal the truth to Lisa about his meetings with McShea.

# Chapter 71

Ryan was shocked that Lisa didn't bother to ask any questions the previous night when McShea called, and he disappeared to his office. Instead, she was curled up with a book in the family room and didn't even look up when he emerged and went upstairs to spend some time with the boys. For all the talk that Ryan has done about ending his cooperation with McShea, it was obvious to her that he still hadn't let go. Eventually, he knew he'd have to come clean with Lisa, but right now he had to sort out this new bombshell that McShea said about Joe Ramos.

Ryan woke the next morning with a new theory about the previous night's call with McShea. *Perhaps McShea wants to use him to put Ramos away.* He jumped out of bed, showered, and dressed quickly. Lisa was at the table in her robe hunched over a bowl of cereal when Ryan walked in and gently kissed her on the cheek.

"Good morning, Lis! No breakfast for me, I forgot that I've got to be in a little early today to assist a new employee on his first day on the job. Might not look good if the new guy is there before me!" Ryan did all he could to avoid a discussion. He grabbed his laptop and flew out the door. Lisa looked over at the freshly baked muffins sitting on the counter and steaming pot of coffee nearby and couldn't recall the last time he'd ever been in that much of a hurry.

The first hour of his day was spent sitting down with the newest member of the team, walking him through the project, required meetings, and the management structure. The rest of the morning was filled with meetings, document reviews, and pesky colleagues poking their heads in the doorway. Late in the afternoon, Ryan thought less about work and more about his meeting that night with McShea. At 4:40 his cell phone began vibrating. The caller ID read *Joe Ramos*. This was exactly what McShea told him might happen.

"Hello?" he said as if he was unaware of who was calling.

"Ryan, this is Joe, Joe Ramos – been quite a while, hope I'm not interrupting you." The voice was friendly and respectful; however, Ryan's guard was up.

"No, that's quite alright. What can I do for you, Joe?"

"If you don't mind me asking, are you still working with FBI agent Mike McShea?" Ramos asked.

*Now why would he want to know that?* Ryan thought. "No, not too much. Helped out with a case here and there but not as much as I helped you." Ryan dangled that out there to see if Ramos would offer any more on why he called.

"Any chance we could meet for a beer sometime this week? Just to chat. Oh, and I'm not asking for any help with anything in case you were wondering," Ramos offered.

"Uh sure, can I get back to you later or tomorrow sometime?" After he ended the conversation, he sat there shaking his head and immediately dialed the number for Mike McShea.

"Hello Mike? You were right – Ramos just called."

"Did he say what he wanted?" McShea asked.

"He wanted to know if I was still working closely with you. I told him, not really. He did say though, that he wanted to meet me sometime this week for a beer to chat. Didn't say about what."

McShea was silent for a moment. "Ryan, why don't you call him back and have him meet you at the warehouse tonight at nine o'clock? Just tell him you don't want to meet in a public place and it's right down from the park you met with him before."

"Yeah, I guess I can do that," Ryan said, a little confused by the request.

"It will be a friendly meeting. I'm curious how he'll react when he sees both of us there. We have to make him believe that it's time to move on and he certainly doesn't need to know that you're going to do one last favor for me. That's between us."

Ryan had no time to think. He hung up and took a deep breath, not sure who to believe or who to trust. He looked at his cell phone and punched in the number for Joe Ramos.

"Well, I didn't expect a call back that quickly!" Ramos said with surprise.

"I know, but I was just getting ready to leave for the day and realized that if we don't meet tonight, I probably can't do it for at least another week or two. Busy work schedule and planning to take the family on a short vacation."

"Tonight's fine. Whatever's convenient for you," Ramos said.

"I've got to be home for a special dinner tonight but can make it later on. Is nine o'clock, okay? I'll be honest, I'd rather that we meet in a non-public place. Remember the park we met at? Well, there's a warehouse, I think it's the Balco warehouse a little way down the road north of the park entrance. Can we meet in that parking lot around nine?"

Ramos hesitated slightly which made Ryan a little uneasy. "Yeah, that sounds fine. I'll see you at nine."

# Chapter 72

The kitchen smelled like Gino's restaurant when Ryan walked through the door after an uneventful day at work. "I could smell the garlic from a block away! Seriously, it smells great in here!" Ryan gushed as he swallowed Lisa up in a bear hug.

"So, how was your day with the new employee?" she asked.

"I think he'll work out just fine. After all, he's got the best mentor in the company," referring to himself.

"That's great, so Joe Farrell is taking him under his wing?" she shot back before they both broke out in a laugh.

Then, Ryan's smile melted away and his brow furrowed. In a sober tone, Ryan confessed that he had received a call from Joe Ramos and was going to meet with him for a few minutes after dinner. He never mentioned anything about Mike McShea.

"I thought you were done with him. Is he asking for help on a case?"

"I don't think so. We had a light-hearted conversation. He just wants to chat. Not sure about what though." Ryan could see by Lisa's smirk that she really wasn't buying it, and to his relief, she didn't push it. She'd wait until he returned home later to get all the details.

***

Shortly after eight, Ryan kissed Lisa goodbye and drove off, still unable to piece together his role in tonight's meeting with Ramos and McShea. He didn't have enough time to even try. The sun had set, and the sky's orange glow was slowly turning dark. By the time he reached the entrance to the Balco warehouse parking lot, darkness had set in. The street was well lit, enough to be able to read the large red letters that spelled out Balco on the side of the warehouse. The chain link fence surrounding the property was in disrepair and covered in overgrown brush and weeds. The narrow entrance from the road led to an unused parking lot at the rear of the property.

Ryan arrived ten minutes early and noticed McShea's car parked awkwardly in the middle of the lot with him outside leaning against the driver's door. McShea motioned for Ryan to park in an unlit area off to the side, away from his car. Ryan did so, turned off his engine and McShea walked toward him.

"Is Ramos coming?" McShea asked.

"He said he'd meet me here at nine. Wanted to have a chat with me and I suspect it has to do with you, since he made it a point to ask if I was still helping you out. So, before he gets here, what is it you wanted to tell me about *him*? You said something about he's not who he says he is?"

"Ryan, he's fooled a lot of people for a long time. His real name is Jose Ramos Alvarez, and he's been in this country illegally after having fled a life of crime in Mexico. He worked for the cartels and may have set up their operation here in the Raleigh area.

"It appeared as though he was sucking you into his organization without you even knowing it. That's why I wanted your assistance just one more time to help put him away. It–"

McShea went silent as a car's headlights could be seen approaching from the side of the warehouse. The pickup's headlights captured the two figures standing in the parking lot as it rolled to a stop a short distance from Ryan's Camry. When Ramos turned off the engine, only the outline of two shadowy figures could be seen and the only sound heard was the hum of an overhead transformer.

Ramos got out and walked across the loose gravel toward them. "Hello Joe," McShea said to a surprised Ramos.

"I wasn't expecting a reunion. Maybe you could tell me what this is all about?" Ramos said looking at both of them.

Ryan put his hands in his pockets and gave a half-hearted shrug, as if asking himself the same thing.

McShea spoke up, sounding somewhat like a teacher lecturing a student. "I was under the impression that you weren't going to bother Mr. Field anymore. He's not a human crystal ball you should be contacting every time you need help solving a crime."

Ramos stiffened and looked sternly at McShea. "Whoa, I had no intention of asking Mr. Field for anything. So, exactly what assistance have *you* been asking for? What sort of cases did Mr. Field assist the Bureau with, or was it only *you* he was assisting?"

Ryan's eyes pulled away from Ramos and locked onto McShea's hand emerging from behind his back with a revolver.

"Unholster your weapon, Mr. Alvarez, and toss it down in front of you," McShea quietly commanded.

"Just as I thought," Ramos said, as he removed the gun from its holster and dropped it in front of him. He straightened, but before he could say another word, McShea fired a shot hitting Ramos in the chest and throwing him onto his back on the gravel.

Ryan gasped, unable to make sense at what just happened.

McShea didn't say anything, as he bent over and picked up Ramos's revolver and coldly stared at Ryan's frightened face.

"Wha-why did–" were the only words Ryan got out before a second shot rang out, striking him in the center of his chest. The shot's force staggered him backwards and he crumpled to the ground.

McShea then calmly removed an envelope containing $5000 from his pocket and placed it in Ryan's limp hand. He pulled out a handkerchief from his back pocket, wiped his prints from Ramos' revolver, and placed it in his lifeless hand. Satisfied that he hadn't missed a detail, he reached for his cell phone and contacted the Raleigh police.

McShea took a deep breath to feign tension in his voice. "This is FBI Agent Mike McShea. I want to report a shooting at the Balco warehouse off Weatherly Road. Both the victim and the suspect are down. I'll remain at the scene until you get here." When several Raleigh police cruisers arrived at the scene, they observed Agent McShea's car in the middle of the parking lot and two other vehicles parked near the fence about twenty feet from each other. The bodies of Ryan Field and Joe Ramos, a.k.a. Jose Alvarez, lay near the parked cars.

Agent Mike McShea stood off to the side, one hand deep in his pocket, the other calmly gesturing as he told his story to the police. "The Fulton cop, Joe Ramos. His real name was Jose Alvarez, and we believe he had ties to Mexican cartels. I believe he was starting to work with Mr. Field, perhaps to expand operations into the Raleigh area. He believed Mr. Ramos to be a friend. When he told me that Ramos wanted to meet him at a warehouse in the evening, it just didn't sound right. I got here as quick as I could." McShea paused and then calmly resumed his story. "You see, Mr. Field was providing me information for my investigation."

"Agent McShea, what was the situation when you arrived on the scene?" asked one of the two officers.

"It was dark, but when I drove into the parking lot, all I saw was Ramos walking quickly toward his car. I didn't see Mr. Field. I got out of my vehicle and called over to Ramos, still unsure of what transpired. He never said a word. He just turned toward me and raised his weapon. That's when I leveled my own revolver and fired off one shot striking him where he stood. I then approached Mr. Field's vehicle and that's when I noticed Mr. Field lying on the ground."

Two more police cruisers arrived on the scene illuminating the warehouse lot in a glow of flashing red and blue. The officers asked McShea for his revolver then walked over to where Joe Ramos was lying on the ground and retrieved his gun as well. One shell casing from each gun found in the area confirmed that each had fired a single shot.

Mike McShea drove home later that evening, pulled a beer out of the fridge, and sat back on the couch with his feet up on the coffee table. He anticipated having no problem painting Joe Ramos as a villain with ties to a drug cartel who had fooled the city of Fulton for a long time. To the very few who were aware of Ryan Field's unique ability, they could be convinced that Ramos may have felt threatened that Ryan would reveal his past. To most, however, it could be argued that Ryan Field simply fell victim to a local cop he thought he knew, not realizing that this cop was not who be pretended to be, but instead, a criminal with ties to drug organizations.

He took a long swig of beer and wiped his mouth with the back of his hand. There was still one very important task remaining on his list to complete - recovering a briefcase hidden away in Alvin Bradford's garage that, as far as he knew, no one except Alvin was aware of its location. With Alvin Bradford behind bars for the next eight years, Agent McShea would have plenty of time to plan a visit to Alvin's garage.

# Chapter 73

Almost a month had passed since the slayings at the Balco warehouse and Lisa Field oscillated between periods of intense grief, anger, and utter confusion, as to how that night could ever have happened. She did her best to shield the boys from all the wild speculation and rumors that circulated about their dad. Many nights, she sat alone in the dark family room, desperately trying to identify what she had missed about "Joe Ramos" and her husband. And she simply couldn't understand how Ryan fit in with all of this, especially considering the news articles reporting that he had been found with a large quantity of cash at the scene.

One afternoon, Lisa received a call from an unexpected source. "Mrs. Field, this is Agent Jared Henderson with the FBI. I want to offer you my sincerest condolences for the passing of your husband."

"Thank you, Agent Henderson. What can I do for you?" Lisa said in a quiet, sad voice. She had never heard Ryan mention this name.

"Mrs. Field, this is not an official call, and it's completely off the record. I've read through the police reports and looked at all the evidence of what happened on that night...with your husband...it just doesn't sit well with me. You see, I worked with Agent McShea; he was at the scene that night." Henderson sensed he had Lisa's full attention.

"Were you with him that night?" Lisa asked.

"No, I wasn't. A while back, Agent McShea had asked me to do an extensive background search of Sergeant Joe Ramos, although he never told me why. Anyway, I found out quite a bit about Ramos's criminal past and that *Joe Ramos* wasn't even his real name. After I provided my findings to Agent McShea, I never heard another word about it. McShea clearly didn't follow up on what I found."

"Did you know that Agent McShea was communicating with my husband?"

"No, but–"

"Agent Henderson, may I ask *you* a question? Exactly what do you know about my husband?" Lisa tried to understand where Agent Henderson fit in and just how much he was aware of.

"Mrs. Field, I never met your husband. One day, I observed a meeting in a local park where agent McShea was meeting up with Joe Ramos. There was a third person present at that meeting which I now believe was your husband. I only knew of your husband through a conversation I had with Joe Ramos one night.

"Wait, so you had discussions with Joe Ramos as well?" Lisa's voice was more pressing now.

"Just *one* discussion. I called him one night for some information. When he heard I was an FBI agent, he got short with me and said he didn't want to discuss anything about *Ryan Field*. I had no clue who Ryan Field was, but there must have been some sort of connection between the two of them. That's the extent of what I knew about your husband. Regarding Joe Ramos and despite what I learned about his past, I found him to be a genuinely likeable person who was devoted to his job." Jared took a deep breath and exhaled loudly.

"And that's why I'm having a hard time with all of this. I've read the police reports. Nothing unusual stands out unless – you happen to personally know the players involved." Jared knew that last statement would provoke her thoughts. It was time for Jared to ask the question that was burning inside of him.

"Mrs. Field, can you tell me what exactly was the relationship between your husband and Joe Ramos? I'm not entirely convinced by what's been reported on the news."

Lisa got up and walked over and eased herself onto the couch in the family room. "Agent Henderson, my husband's gone, but there was something very special about him; something you may find hard, if not impossible, to believe. One day he woke up just like any other day and told me about a dream he had had the night before. In his dream, he witnessed the abduction of a little girl and observed all the details surrounding it. As he told me this, I happened to be reading a story about a little girl who was abducted from her driveway two days earlier on the other side of town. The description of the girl matched what my husband saw in his dream. The police had no clues and no suspects."

"And Sgt. Ramos?" Jared asked.

"I'll get to that in a moment. My husband, Ryan, thought this might be just a coincidence so, later that day he drove by the home of where the abduction took place. The home, the driveway, and even the tree that he stood near in his dream were identical to what he saw that day. When he got back home, he stretched out on the bed to think about what he had just seen. He fell asleep and when he woke, he told me that he witnessed the abduction again!"

"Mrs. Field, it's not uncommon for people to read about something or perhaps see something on the nightly news and then have that be a part of their dreams." Jared's tone was gentle yet condescending.

Lisa straightened, and her voice was a little more forceful. "Agent Henderson, perhaps you didn't hear what I said earlier. There were no suspects or witnesses. My husband saw a van, a suspect, and witnessed the entire abduction. He provided details of the van and a description of the suspect to the Fulton police department. That day, the little girl was found, and the suspect was arrested because of the anonymous tip my husband provided! A tip that was provided to Sgt. Joe Ramos."

"Whoa! So, why an anonymous tip to Sgt. Ramos?" Jared asked, adding another piece to the puzzle.

"It *had* to be anonymous. How could he ever explain knowing the identity of the suspect and the vehicle when there were no known witnesses? And this wasn't a one-time thing. He called in multiple tips to help solve crimes that the police couldn't."

"So, why Sgt. Ramos?" Jared persisted.

"We knew Sgt. Ramos for several years through community events, and he was always very friendly and trustworthy. Although Ryan felt comfortable providing him the anonymous tips, he was still hesitant to identify himself. One day though, Ryan got a call from Sergeant Ramos, who somehow figured out where the tips were coming from. As far as I know, this was all kept just between the two of them."

"Did Ryan have any idea of Ramos's past?"

Lisa sounded tired. "I honestly don't know. After a while, he didn't talk as much about his dreams and sometimes after dinner he'd just disappear into his office for hours."

"Did your husband have many dreams about crimes, and did they all turn out to have really happened?"

Lisa sensed that Jared Henderson still had his doubts about Ryan's ability and tried to attribute Ryan's dreams to events that he either witnessed or read about somewhere, without really remembering that he had done so.

"Agent Henderson, it was more than just waking from a dream and relating it to something that had already happened."

"How so?"

"Ryan realized that if he started to concentrate on the details of a specific location, date, and time, that he could fall asleep and he'd be there. Do you understand what I'm telling you? He could place himself at a location in the past and observe whatever it is that took place." Lisa could barely hear Jared breathing on the other end.

"Wait – you mean he could go back in time, witness something, and remember the details when he woke up?"

"Exactly! And that's why Ryan didn't want any of this getting out. Most people would have labeled him as delusional, a nut case. And just imagine the demands that would have been put on him by law enforcement agencies, parents with missing children, reporters –

you name it. Ryan felt overwhelmed by it and after helping with a few local cases with Joe Ramos, he really wanted it all to stop. And then one day, he came home and said that Joe Ramos introduced him to Agent Mike McShea to help with a few FBI cases. That was the last Ryan heard from Joe Ramos, until that is, the night that bastard murdered my husband."

Jared hung his head and quietly spoke. "Mrs. Field, I am so sorry for what happened to your husband. You've been very gracious in helping me to understand a little more about what's happened. I won't take up any more of your time." After he hung up the phone, Jared Henderson looked down at the notes he had been furiously taking during the call – *Ramos introduced Ryan to McShea, Ryan could place himself in a specific location at a specific time*? For several minutes he stared at the words.

"Ramos and Ryan Field dead. And McShea happened to be there? Nope, I'm not buying this," he uttered in a barely audible voice.

# Chapter 74

FBI Agent Mike McShea had compiled a substantial file of his carefully constructed "investigation" into Joe Ramos, which he was confident would lead to the arrest of a popular officer in the Fulton police department. His superiors and local law enforcement accepted McShea's report without question and concluded that he had acted responsibly and with just cause in the shooting of Sergeant Joe Ramos, formerly known as Jose Alvarez. The case was eventually considered closed by both the Raleigh Police and the FBI.

Meanwhile, McShea's routine and demeanor around the office never wavered. He still carried himself with a quiet arrogance and maintained his preference to work behind the closed door of his office. His thoughts though, drifted far from Raleigh and often landed him on a warm beach, especially when reclining in his chair gazing at the picture of that sleek Bertram cabin cruiser on the wall in front of him.

He had begun taking weekend fishing trips to the Outer Banks, usually on the third weekend of the month, allowing himself to be seduced by the sounds of circling sea gulls and waves slapping against the bow. He was sure he could live comfortably off his pension and the financial assets he had acquired with the help of Ryan Field, although one of those assets was still out there tucked away in a garage waiting for him.

On the Friday night of one of his fishing weekends, McShea made a planned detour to a small home in Garner, a town southeast of Raleigh. He parked a block away and walked along the dark, narrow roadway until he reached the home where Alvin Bradford had lived prior to his incarceration. Alvin's mother, the only other occupant in the house, worked the nightshift at Waffle House and wouldn't be home until eight o'clock the next morning. Mike

McShea had meticulously planned this visit to access the garage at the end of the driveway and retrieve the briefcase that had been left there months earlier.

With the briefcase secured in the trunk of his car, McShea took the main highway out of Garner and resumed his trip to the Outer Banks. The arrogance surfaced on his face as he pictured the look on Alvin Bradford's face after he's released from prison to reunite with his stolen cash, only to find an empty shelf. With this asset secured, McShea turned his thoughts to retirement, fishing, and the beautiful boat he'd own.

***

Lisa Field reconstructed her life as a widow with her two fatherless boys. There was an outpouring of support from neighbors and members of the community, many of whom she didn't know. Life at home changed drastically. The boys didn't go out as much and elected to spend more time home with their mother. Dinnertime had lost that ring of laughter from the dumb jokes and the crazy stories from school. The boys would still disappear upstairs after dinner, but Lisa would find it hard to settle on the couch in the family room, as she once did with Ryan. Most nights she'd venture into the office and read through the notes and files Ryan had kept of his dreams and the specific cases he had helped Joe Ramos with. The tears continued to flow, and she did her best to hide that from the boys. Often, she blamed herself for encouraging Ryan to trust his secret with the sergeant from the Fulton police department. She still didn't fully understand the relationship between Ryan and Joe Ramos, or why he chose to kill her husband. How could she have been so wrong?

# Chapter 75

Four years had passed since Jason and Aaron Field lost their dad. Jason was now in high school and just started driving. Aaron, who was three years younger than Jason, had experienced a growth spurt and was now the same height as his brother. Lisa Field managed an antique shop in downtown Fulton, just a short walk away from the police department. Weekday mornings at the Field house were hectic, as the two boys prepared for school and Lisa got ready for work. Lisa, though, insisted on one thing in the morning – that they all sit down and have breakfast together.

October was a week old, and the sun had yet to make an appearance. The light hanging over the kitchen table was turned up. Three glasses of orange juice sat on the table, each in front of a placemat with a neatly placed knife and fork. The strong scent of bacon pierced the air, as Lisa emptied the frying pan of scrambled eggs into a large bowl. She didn't have to yell upstairs for the boys to come down; the smell wafting up from the kitchen was enough.

"Mornin' Mom!" Aaron said, as he rushed to sit down. "Is it okay if Reed's mom drives me home today after practice?"

"Sure, just let me know if you're going to be home later than six," Lisa said as she walked the bowl of scrambled eggs to the table.

Jason was still combing his wet hair when he entered the kitchen, but Lisa noticed a puzzling look on his face as he sat down. "You sleep ok?" she asked.

"Yeah, I slept fine... had a really weird dream though. I was in the school parking lot and watched Johnny Akers and Carl Marrone slash the tires of the assistant principal's car. And here's the crazy part – two weeks ago, the assistant principal's tires *were* slashed in the parking lot, and they still don't know who did it. Weird huh?" Jason just shook his head and started to eat.

Lisa covered her mouth and turned away, trying to appear calm.

The boys soon finished their breakfast and headed out the door for school. Lisa remained at the table wide-eyed, staring at them at the end of the driveway. After a moment, she reached over for her iPhone and searched for the number of the Raleigh FBI office. She took a deep breath, exhaled, and punched in the number.

"Agent Jared Henderson, please."

## ABOUT THE AUTHOR

James Wittenborg is a first-time novelist and long-time member of the space community. A senior systems engineer with a Masters in Space Studies, he began his career manning the console at Houston's Mission Control Center in support of the Space Shuttle Program test flights. He went on to support the initial development of the International Space Station (ISS) in Reston Virginia, then on to the Canadian Space Agency in St. Hubert, Quebec where he worked in the operations organization for the ISS robotic Canadarm. Currently, he supports the Space Launch System for the Artemis Program in Huntsville, Alabama, where he resides with his wife, Kathy. He has three grown children, Karine, Victoria, and Christopher.

Made in the USA
Columbia, SC
19 February 2023

12358615R00120